Kent leaned toward her, placing a finger under Jill's chin and tipping her face up toward him. "Your eyes are shining," he said. "Do you think that's passion, Amaretto or just reflected firelight?"

"Probably insanity," she returned.

"Mmm." He observed her with amusement. "And just how insane are you, my dear?" Before she could respond, his lips brushed against her cheek, then slid quickly and firmly to her mouth.

As she slipped her arms around him and returned his kiss with growing desire, it occurred to Jill momentarily that she ought to draw away—it was dangerous being here alone late at night. But it was a moment that might never come again. Whatever it cost her, she couldn't bear to lose it.

The Dream Never Dies

JACQUELINE DIAMOND P₂

A Love Affair from

HARLEQUIN

London · Toronto · New York · Sydney

First published in Great Britain in 1985 by
Harlequin, 15–16 Brook's Mews, London W1A 1DR

© Jackie Hyman 1984

ISBN 0 373 16079 8

18-0985

Printed and bound in Great Britain by
Richard Clay (The Chaucer Press) Ltd,
Bungay, Suffolk

Chapter One

Jill Brandon felt a thrill of excitement mixed with apprehension as she turned her Dart into the parking lot of the *Daily Journal-Review*. It was housed in a sprawling, one-story building too small for printing presses, but she already knew they shared those with another paper. As she halted in a space marked Visitors, she glanced at the stack of marked-up newspapers on the passenger seat beside her.

During her years of reporting and editing, she'd gravitated more and more toward design, both of the physical appearance of the paper and the content. Gradually she'd come to feel frustration at having to work within limits set by other people, frequently without much thought or knowledge. Now, as a newspaper consultant, it was her job to reshape other people's papers.

Jill scooped up the stack of *Daily Journal*s and her briefcase and slid out of the car. She didn't usually feel this nervous on beginning a new assignment, but ever since she'd read the masthead on the editorial page, she'd known this job would be a challenge personally as well as professionally.

You look just fine, she told herself as she strode firmly up the sidewalk toward the entrance. She knew the crisp linen suit was both businesslike and feminine, and the soft blue silk blouse set off her amber eyes and chestnut hair. At twenty-nine, she'd changed considerably since her scruffy reporting days ... Well, no use thinking about that.

She stepped into the spacious lobby, noting with some amazement that there was no variation in temperature from outside. It was one of the things she still hadn't gotten used to since moving to Southern California last year. Having grown up in the Midsouth, she had assumed that everywhere the summers were hot and muggy and the winters brief but snapping cold. Instead, here the temperature seemed stuck at seventy-two.She had to think for a minute before remembering it was October.

She inquired at the desk and was asked to wait for the publisher's secretary. Sitting on a plastic-upholstered chair, she watched the receptionists answer the switchboard and direct visitors to the classified advertising section.

Trying to keep her thoughts on a neutral topic, Jill decided to spend part of the weekend exploring

Buena Park. She'd never been here before, and since she'd luckily arranged to apartment-sit while her friend Lanni was in Europe, she wouldn't have to keep driving back to her own apartment in West Los Angeles. Besides, although the *Daily Journal* was expanding to compete with other papers in Orange County, it still basically served its home-town, and she wanted to try to learn more about the community.

A young woman with free-flowing blond hair walked toward her with an inquiring glance. "Are you Miss Brandon?" she asked.

"Yes, I am." Jill stood up and shook hands.

"I'm Cindy Selby, Mr. Latimore's secretary," the other woman said with a self-conscious grin. She didn't look more than twenty-one or twenty-two and was wearing a casual jump suit, but Jill supposed that Mr. Latimore, having just taken over as editor and publisher, hadn't had time to seek out an experienced secretary.

She followed Cindy across the lobby. As they passed through an outer office, Jill noticed the secretary's desk was covered with a disarray of papers and edged by an assortment of slogans and gnome figures.

The inner office, by contrast, was subdued and plush. A trim, silver-haired man rose to greet her. "I'm Arnold Latimore," he said, acknowledging Cindy's introduction and offering Jill a seat and a low table for her stack of papers. "Coffee? We have our own pot down here; the stuff in the machines is awful."

"Sounds just like a newspaper," Jill grinned, and the publisher smiled back warmly.

As soon as Cindy had departed for the coffee, he settled down behind his desk. "I'm impressed by your credentials, Miss Brandon," he said. "By the way, can we be on a first-name basis? I'm from Boston myself and used to a little more formality than you find in California, but we'll be working together for a few weeks and I'd like us both to feel comfortable."

"That's fine with me," Jill said. "I know some people might think I was treading on their toes, especially since it was Coastal Communications Group that brought me in."

"I think you'll find we're on the same side." Arnold leaned back in his chair. He looked quite distinguished in his three-piece suit, but more like a businessman than an editor. "As you know, CCG just bought the *Journal* a few months back, and we're getting ready to mount a circulation drive."

"I take it I'm part of the campaign," Jill said.

"That's right. We're bringing people in to analyze our classified and display ads and circulation department, but it all boils down to the news product. If people don't like what they see, they won't buy the paper, and we've got some heavy competition."

"How does your staff feel about my being here?" She tried not to show how important the answer was.

"Oh, they're a little wary, which I guess is natural," Arnold said. "First I come in here and now you. People tend to get set in their ways of doing things, even though this is the second time the paper's been sold in four years."

"I have to admit I was surprised to hear about it," Jill said. "The previous owner—Michael Arbizzi, isn't that his name?—had done such a good job of taking a biweekly and building it up."

"Frankly, he wouldn't have sold it if it hadn't been for his heart attack," Arnold said. "This is a good little paper, and CCG knows it. We're going to make it a good, big paper."

After a quick knock, Cindy shuffled in with two cups of coffee. She'd tucked sugar and packets of powdered creamer in her pockets and brought them out crumpled.

After she departed, Arnold shrugged apologetically. "I inherited her with the job; she still acts like a college kid, which is what she was not long ago, but one of the conditions of sale was that we keep the staff members in their jobs, unless there's good cause to fire them, of course. I keep hoping she'll shape up."

There was no avoiding the next question, so Jill swallowed hard and tried to make her tone casual.

"You haven't mentioned the managing editor. Do you think he'll be hard to work with?"

"Kent?" Arnold said. "Well, as a matter of fact, when I noticed you used to work in Nashville, I thought maybe you knew him."

"I do. He used to be my assignment editor." Amazing how matter-of-fact her voice sounded, Jill thought. "I don't suppose he'll be too eager about having his former kid reporter come in and change things around."

"He understands the importance—" The telephone interrupted, and Arnold picked it up with a look of annoyance. "Cindy, I thought I told you ... Oh, all right."

As he talked, Jill's thoughts defied her resolve and settled on Kent Lawrence. She remembered quite clearly the first time she'd seen him eight years before.

It had been her first reporting job, right out of college, and she was trying to hide her trembling as she was introduced to the assignment editor. Her anxiety hadn't been lessened by his powerfully masculine good looks. As he stood to greet her, she saw that he was tall with broad shoulders and a lean, hard body. He'd been distracted, hardly noticing her, but she'd found herself mesmerized by the deep blue eyes against the rugged, bronze skin. Then he'd turned away rapidly to grab a ringing phone, snapping an order at a copyboy and marking up a story with a blue pen even while he talked. With an inward sigh she'd taken the stack of rewrites he tossed at her and gone to her desk.

Only her determination to succeed had enabled Jill to overcome her fear of him those next weeks. Kent seemed to find endless faults in her copy, and several times she barely escaped to the rest room in time to hide her tears. Then she realized that he treated all reporters that way, and finally, when she began receiving a sprinkling of compliments along with the criticisms, she relaxed.

It was hard to say when he'd begun to notice her as a woman; probably the election night they both worked late and then went out for coffee. He was only six years older than she was, Jill realized. Furthermore, having been transplanted to Nashville from California, he had no family or longtime friends around and little time to socialize. They'd talked for several hours and parted reluctantly, but the next morning he'd barked at her as gruffly as ever.

A week later they ran into each other by accident at a bar that specialized in bluegrass music. She turned and stopped, an electric jolt going through her at the tender expression in those intense blue eyes. When he caught her gaze, he tried to nod indifferently, then shrugged and gave up. They spent the rest of the evening talking.

He followed her home, saying it was late and he wanted to be sure she made it safely. But somehow when he walked her to her door, they couldn't part with a simple good night. He touched her shoulders lightly, then ran his hands down her arms. She tingled at his touch, feeling her breath come more quickly as he bent over and brushed her lips with his. Her hands ruffled through his soft sandy hair, and then they were clinging together, his firm hard body against her rounded, yielding one, sharing a deep kiss that sent flames licking through her.

It had been no use pretending their relationship was a casual one. After that, they'd seen each other regularly, carefully keeping their meetings secret from their co-workers. They'd planned to take jobs in another city and marry, until...

"Sorry about that," Arnold said, hanging up the phone. "It's like a madhouse around here."

"I don't want to take up too much of your time," Jill said. "What I'd appreciate is for you to tell me what you want from me, and then I'd like to meet the staff and talk with the editors individually."

"Fine." Arnold rested his elbows on the desk, interlacing his fingers and frowning in thought. "I'll be frank about this. I come from the business side of newspapers, not the editorial side. I don't know much about content; I leave that to the managing editor. But I know that we're competing not only with other newspapers but with television and radio and magazines. People want to have their attention grabbed; they want to see something visually exciting. I want our paper to give them that."

Jill nodded. She suspected already that Arnold and Kent must have their share of disagreements; Kent was a stickler for accuracy and thoroughness, which meant longer articles. But the two viewpoints didn't have to be incompatible.

"I think you're talking about packaging," she said and was pleased to see him nod appreciatively. Buzzwords like packaging were especially important to business people, she'd learned. "I've been studying the *Journal* and I think you've got some good writers and good ideas, which is the basis. After all, I think you'll agree that no matter how exciting a paper looks, if it's boring to read, people won't subscribe."

"Well, yes, of course."

"I have some ideas for dressing up some of the sections and reshuffling things a bit," Jill said. "I'd like to discuss these with the staff to get their input, but, well, for example, there's entertainment scattered all over the paper. Articles in the features section, in the Sunday section, in the run-of-press"—she saw his blank look and explained—"the inside news pages. It doesn't seem to be well-coordinated; there's some duplication. I think that should be centralized."

"Well, that's a good point..." He wasn't responding with much enthusiasm.

"I'm sure you're aware that movie theaters are

one of a paper's biggest advertisers," she said and saw his eyes light up. "But as I said, I want to meet with the staff before I draw up my proposals. And I'll need to see a printout of the typefaces in your computer."

"Oh, sure, I'll introduce you to Pete Alcala. He's the head of the back shop," Arnold said. "Well, let's go on up and say hello to Kent, and then I'll let yóu get to work."

She left her papers with Cindy and followed tensely as Arnold led her past the advertising departments to the city room. How would Kent react on seeing her again? What did he look like now? Was he married? Maybe he'd forgotten her . . . .

The newsroom looked like every other one she'd seen: large and rectangular, with clusters of file cabinets scattered throughout and rows of desks fanning out from the copydesk area. Separate groupings along three of the walls probably represented the sports, features, and Sunday sections, she guessed, noticing at the same time that the faint click of word processors—CRTs, for cathode ray tubes—had replaced the clatter of typewriters so familiar from her reporting days.

Arnold guided her through the desks to an office on the far side of the room. On her way Jill noticed the curious glances directed at her by people sitting at various points. No doubt they'd heard she was coming and were curious and possibly a little apprehensive. There were always one or two strongly resistant ones but, she hoped, not too many.

The publisher stepped aside and let her enter the open office door first. Kent, sitting at his desk looking over the early edition, glanced up.

An expression of surprise spread over his face, and for a moment he didn't move. He hadn't changed much, Jill noted. If anything, the few additional lines added to the impression of rugged masculinity.

"I think you two know each other," Arnold said, startling her back to the present.

"Yes." The blue eyes were hooded as he rose politely. "It's been a long time, Miss Brandon."

"Jill," she said, accepting a seat.

"Jill's with the Newspaper Design Center," Arnold said.

Once again, Kent's handsome face revealed astonishment. "Our consultant?"

Arnold nodded. "I'll let you two get down to business. Jill knows what I'm looking for. I'll speak to Pete about the typefaces," he told her. "Seems to me we've got a book of them somewhere. Let me know how it's going."

"Of course," Jill said. She tried to steady her breathing as he left, then turned to Kent. "I thought you knew I was coming."

"I knew we were getting a consultant, but I didn't know whom." Instead of sitting, he walked past her and stood in the doorway, looking out at

the newsroom. What was he thinking? she wondered. Perhaps he was remembering the day of
their first serious quarrel, when she'd proposed to
go undercover as a newly arrived, would-be country singer for an investigative series into rumors
that such dewy-eyed girls were being lured into
prostitution.

He'd turned her down coldly, and she'd been
furious. Kent didn't have enough faith in her as a
reporter, and the result would be to limit her career. Or maybe he thought she'd chicken out if
there was trouble; she insisted she had as much
courage as any male reporter. Besides, she was
sure nothing serious would happen. They'd ar-
gued for days, at work and in private.

Kent interrupted her memories by returning to
his chair. "You've certainly come a long way," he
said. "I've followed your career in the professional
journals. Quite an impressive string of credits."

"Thank you." Jill didn't want to admit she
hadn't been reading the trade publications herself
until recently, perhaps because she was afraid that
she'd learn he was married. She was relieved to
see he wore no ring. Then she chided herself.
What difference could it make?

"You were always ambitious," Kent went on.
"You seem to have the game plan all worked out.
Your next step I suppose will be a top editing position on a major paper or at least one that's growing rapidly, won't it?"

"I haven't really thought about that." She had to fight the feeling of being a young, inexperienced woman, just as she'd been when she'd last seen him seven years before. His tone was ironic, almost angry, and she felt the tears prickle near the surface. *Stop it*, Jill told herself. *The two of us have to work together, and I'm just as much a professional as he is.*

"Let's get one thing clear," Kent said. "I may have been a stepping-stone for you once, but it isn't going to be that way again."

"Kent, you were never..."

"Let me finish." His eyes glittered angrily. "This is my newspaper. I came here because Michael Arbizzi and I were old friends, and when he bought the *Journal-Review*, it was my chance to do what I'd always wanted: have a paper of my own, that I cared about, that meant something. Well, unfortunately, he's had to sell out, but I've spent the last four years of my life building this newspaper into something I'm proud of, and I'm not going to turn it into the journalistic equivalent of *People* magazine."

"It's nice to know what you think of my integrity as a newspaperwoman," she snapped.

"I don't know much about your integrity," he answered coldly. "I do know about your ambition, and there's a lot of interest in what happens to the *Journal*. There hasn't been a real circulation war around here since before anyone can remember, and we're going up against a paper that's a lot bigger and a lot better established.''

"And you propose to win that war on content alone?" she asked.

"I don't care what kind of gimmicks the advertising people use," Kent retorted, leaning forward and glaring at her. "But what's printed in the news pages is my business."

"Nobody's disputing your ability as an editor," Jill said. "But there are a lot of things that can be improved without sacrificing quality. I'm not a kid reporter anymore, Kent. I've worked at some top newspapers, and I know what I'm doing. Your logos and headline styles are out-of-date. The layouts are haphazard; one day they're pretty good, the next day they're awful. You're not packaging the news as well as you could. The features section..." She stopped herself, infuriated by her own hotheadedness. She hadn't meant to throw everything at him.

To her astonishment, he broke into a grin. "Well, I'm pleasantly surprised," he said.

"That I know something about my business?"

"Hell no. I expected that." He leaned back in his chair. "That you got angry. Here I thought you'd turned into a cold-blooded executive, and I find you still have a temper."

"Just because a woman isn't a doormat doesn't make her cold-blooded," Jill shot back.

"You were certainly never a doormat," he said. "Shall I show you around?"

"Sure." She rose hesitantly, surprised by the change in his manner. He touched her elbow to guide her out of the office, and a thrill ran through her at his touch. *What's wrong with me?* she demanded. She knew they weren't suited to each other. She'd found out a long time ago he didn't really want her to be herself, hadn't she?

It was almost three o'clock and, since the *Journal* was an afternoon paper, most of the copydesk had gone to lunch. Off deadline, the reporters were mostly out in the field, with only a few pecking determinedly away at their CRTs. The atmosphere was listless, nothing like the newsrooms one saw on television, but Jill knew how electrically alive everything could become with a single phone call, one dramatic bit of breaking news. A plane crash, a death ... Despite the tragedy of so much of what a reporter wrote about, she sometimes missed being right there in the middle of the action.

"Frank Rickles, our sports editor." Jill shook hands with a short, wiry man of indeterminate age, who greeted her warmly.

"About time somebody knocked this rag into shape!" he chortled with a sly look at Kent.

"The only thing wrong with the *Journal* is the sports section," the managing editor joked back.

"These guys are small potatoes. They're great on underwater paraplegic polo, but ever since the Angels and the Rams moved to Orange County, they've been out of their depth."

"I can see you guys really hit it off," Jill smiled. "I'm a Dodgers fan myself, but I try to keep my biases out of my work."

"Well, they're not a bad team," Frank acknowledged. "You're not so bad yourself. You really dress this place up. We old bachelors will have to look out, won't we, Kent?"

Jill was relieved when a voice from the back shop squawked Frank's name over an intercom, and the sports editor had to excuse himself to go check a page proof. She glanced at Kent, but he merely chuckled and led the way to another cluster of desks.

Mary Jane Kincaid, the Sunday editor, was a pleasant woman of about fifty, slightly stocky and unpretentious. Jill liked her at once.

"Your headlines are delightful," Jill said. "I noticed some wonderful puns."

Mary Jane accepted the compliment graciously. "I do my best," she said. "I've got a great staff."

"I could tell," Jill said. "I'll want to talk with all of you to get your ideas. I hope you don't think I've come here to steamroller over you. What I'd like best is to build on the talents and interests of the people who are here."

"It's always helpful to get some objective criticism," Mary Jane said. "I think we tend to get a little set in our ways. There are a few areas I think could be improved, but I wasn't sure how to go about it. I'll look forward to talking with you."

Jill felt relieved as they walked away. Both Frank and Mary Jane struck her as competent and easy to work with.

"I'll say one thing, you can certainly turn on the charm when you want to," Kent said.

"Hey! What's that supposed to mean?"

He looked surprised. "It was intended as a compliment. I'm glad to see your success hasn't turned you into a snob."

"You act as though my real personality was obnoxious and I just manage to cover it up," Jill answered.

"You're overreacting," Kent said. "Now don't argue. Here's our features editor, Anita Ruiz. Anita, this is Jill Brandon, our consultant."

"How do you do." Anita, a statuesque brunette with sultry dark eyes and a soft, clinging dress that emphasized her curvaceous figure, gave Jill a look of veiled hostility.

"I'm pleased to meet you," Jill said. It wasn't really true; Anita's was the weakest section of the paper, with sloppy editing both of copy and of page proofs, and Jill had been afraid she'd run up against her strongest opposition here of any of the special sections. That seemed to be the case.

"By the way"—Anita turned to Kent and her

tone sweetened—"you haven't forgotten about the Press Club party this evening? We've worked so hard, and I've promised that the whole *Journal* will turn up."

"It's the Halloween party," Kent informed Jill, then addressed Anita. "Of course I'm going; you know how I love parties." His tone was ironic, but the features editor only laughed.

"Oh, you're crusty, but I know you're a softy underneath." She winked and Kent looked slightly embarrassed. Jill felt uncomfortable. She didn't really think there was anything going on between the two, or Anita wouldn't have been flirting so openly, but the woman was extremely attractive and was making no secret of her interest in Kent.

"As a matter of fact, I thought it might be a good idea if Jill came along," Kent said. "It'll give her a chance to meet the rest of the staff and for us all to get comfortable with each other. She needs to hear all our griping so she knows where we're coming from."

"Oh, I'm sure she's not one of those women who feels she has to work all the time," Anita countered with barely concealed annoyance. "She's probably already made plans for tonight."

"Well, no. Actually it sounds like a good idea." Jill didn't want to antagonize the woman, but it seemed inevitable anyway, and she hadn't been looking forward to spending Friday night alone in a strange apartment. She felt unsettled at the thought of spending the evening with Kent, but no doubt he just planned to introduce her around and then let her make her own way.

"Well, looks like the copydesk is wandering back in, so I'd better go make introductions," Kent said, pulling Jill away by the arm. Anita said a frosty good-bye.

"Why did you suggest I go to the party?" Jill inquired. "It was obvious she didn't want me."

"It isn't her party; she's just on the committee," Kent said. "I meant what I said about your meeting the staff. Like it or not, we've got to work together. Or did you have plans for tonight?"

"No..." She let him guide her through the clutter of desks.

"If you did, I suspect the poor guy knows your job comes first," Kent said, his expression suddenly stern.

"Kent, I wish you wouldn't keep implying I'm some kind of dragon lady. Just because I'm good at what I do..."

They reached the copydesk area, and she bit off the words as Kent made another round of introductions. In the blur of faces, she picked out the chubby copy chief and another copy editor who doubled as the business page editor. The city editor, Lewis France, a thirtyish man with a reserved manner, greeted her politely. Jill was relieved when they continued on toward the back shop.

A long corridor gave them a chance to talk with

some privacy about Nashville. "Kent," she said, deciding to get their previous conflict out into the open, "when I mentioned that investigative series to the managing editor, I honestly never meant..."

"We've been through all that," Kent said tautly. "He just happened to compliment you on a story you'd done, and you just happened to mention this idea you had about aspiring country singers that the assignment editor had turned down."

"All right, I admit it wasn't entirely innocent," Jill said. "Sure I wanted a chance to show what I could do. I thought you were being unfair. And you were, Kent! I proved that!"

"You proved a lot of things," he said, and once again deftly sidestepped her response by halting to introduce her to a woman who was walking toward them. "This is Kay Martin, our art director."

Jill was already having trouble sorting out her impressions of all the people she'd met, and the problem only grew worse as they met more of the heads of advertising and promotional departments, then progressed through the back shop with its welter of paste-up tables and typesetting computers. Kent even knew the typists and proofreaders by name.

"Couldn't I meet the rest on Monday?" she asked as they paused to look at a computer that was spewing out a punched tape that another machine would translate into type. "My head is spinning."

"Sure," Kent said. "Actually you've just about met everybody, and it's time for our story conference. I know you won't want to miss that."

"Why would you have a story conference on a Friday afternoon?" she asked, trying to keep up with his rapid stride back toward the newsroom. She knew the *Journal* would probably already have most of the inside pages for Saturday, Sunday, and Monday already laid out.

"This is our daily meeting—something I initiated," Kent said over his shoulders, apparently not noticing her exertions. "When we first went daily, all we had was quick once-over at the copydesk in the morning, and half the time we didn't know what the features section was doing."

"I don't suppose you talk about entertainment stories at these conferences?" Jill panted.

"Not unless they're staff-written, but you're right; we had two different wire stories on the same subject last week." Kent slowed down, his tanned face thoughtful. "I'll admit there are some weaknesses."

"We can work together peacefully, can't we?" Jill asked. The sudden awareness of his physical presence as they strolled alone down the corridor made her feel weak. Kent was, if anything, even more attractive than he'd been seven years ago. His body was slim and well-muscled; he'd always been an avid tennis player, and here, no doubt, he played all year round. In addition, he'd gained in self-assurance, a certain masculine awareness that struck an immediate responsive chord in her.

I've grown, too, but probably not in ways he would appreciate, she thought ruefully as they drew closer to the newsroom. The qualities she prized in herself—confidence, professionalism, strength—unquestionably merited his respect, but she realized with a pang that she wanted more from him, even after all these years. Yet what he wanted, if he wanted anything from her, was that uncertain, wide-eyed cub reporter, a young woman she could never be again.

Most of the editors had already gathered in the conference room adjacent to Kent's office, a place he indicated Jill could use as her base of operations during her weeks at the *Journal*. It was a modest-sized room with a long table that seated about a dozen people and some shelves at the side where she could store her marked-up papers and notes, although she planned to keep most of them in her briefcase.

Frank and Mary Jane greeted her warmly, and she received a cordial nod from the city editor, Lewis France. Anita Ruiz, pouring herself a cup of coffee from the sideboard, appeared not to notice her.

"Where's Arnold?" Kent asked.

"On his way," said Mary Jane. "Gidget called

over to say she dropped her tuna fish sandwich on the floor just as he came out of his office and he took a skid. Had to have his wife drop off a change of pants."

There was an appreciative chuckle from the group. Jill had to admit Gidget was an appropriate nickname for Cindy.

"It's getting to be like the Marx Brothers in there," said Frank, twiddling a nonexistent mustache.

Their comments were cut off as Arnold marched in, looking a bit sheepish, followed by a very abashed Cindy. She perched at one end of the table and began doodling on her secretarial pad.

Arnold took a seat by Jill, favoring her with a warm smile. Glancing up, she caught the edge of a frown on Kent's face, but he quickly assumed a blank, editor-in-charge look.

"Well, what've we got for the weekend and Monday?" he began. "And what are we looking at for next week?" Jill wished she could have started at the *Journal* on a Monday, instead of having one day and then an interruption, but Arnold had been out of town early in the week and hadn't been free until today.

The editors ran through their offerings. The most interesting one came from Anita, although the features editor didn't seem to realize it.

"We've got a story I've been holding until I had enough space," she said casually. "It's about a pair of grown-up Siamese twins. There's some interesting art with it." Jill mentally translated art into photographs.

"You mean these people are still attached?" asked the city editor.

Anita nodded. "Yes. Apparently there was too great a chance of their dying if they were separated, so their parents decided against it. They're twenty-five now, nice-looking guys, too, except they're joined at the chest. They only have one heart."

"How long have you been sitting on this?" Kent's tone was deceptively quiet.

"Oh, about a week," Anita said, batting her dark eyelashes up at him. She looked striking, her dark skin glowing against her scarlet silk dress, although Jill thought she wore a bit too much eye makeup.

Kent turned to Mary Jane. "What kind of space have you got left on Sunday?"

"At this point we've already shot the whole Today section," she said. "Our page-one special is on the opening of the new cancer research center next week; I'm afraid we're kind of locked into that."

"Damn," Kent muttered. "I don't want to waste this on a Saturday. All right, Anita, turn over the story and the art to Lewis. We'll feature it Monday on the front page, jumping to page three."

"If you do that, what am I going to put in my section?" Anita complained; then, finally realizing Kent was angry, she muttered quickly, "Oh, that's all right. I'll find something."

"You do that," said the managing editor coldly. "All right. Anything else?" When no one answered, he dismissed the meeting.

Arnold turned to Jill. "You know, it just occurred to me, there's a Halloween Press Club party tonight. It might give you a chance to get to know everybody better. My wife refuses to go to those things; so if you'd like an escort, I'd be more than happy to oblige."

"She's going with me." At Kent's words, Arnold looked up and the two men locked gazes. Jill sensed their real battle had nothing to do with her, and she hoped she wasn't going to end up in the middle of it.

"Guess I'll have to take a rain check," Arnold said at last, his inflection casual. He smiled down at Jill as he rose. "Have a good time, and we'll see you on Monday. I'd like to talk with you then."

"Of course." Jill stood up. "I'll drop in to see you at your convenience."

He left, Cindy hurrying after him.

"Looks like you've made a conquest," said Kent, a trace of contempt in his voice.

"You must be out of your mind if you think I'd chase after a married man," she snapped.

"I don't think anything of the kind." He met

her eyes coolly. "But we know how good you are at currying favor with those in power, where your career is concerned."

"Kent..."

But he'd already walked by her and was on his way out of the conference room.

Chapter Two

Jill hesitated, trying to get her emotions under control. It was unjust of Kent to keep needling her and then preventing her from responding. She remembered him as being much gentler, listening to her carefully; but she had to remind herself that that had been in their private relationship, not at work.

I've got to keep this strictly business, she told herself. *Otherwise I might get so tangled up in my feelings it'll interfere with my work.*

Despite her dedication to her career, Jill had certainly not cut herself off from men over the years, but she'd learned long ago to be very careful to keep them separate from her work.

Kent had been the first lesson, and a very strong one. Ever since her special project was approved by the managing editor, he'd been so frosty to her that they'd gradually stopped seeing each other. Matters had worsened as she got deeper into her research, making friends with some young hopeful singers and hanging around with them.

One night she and two other women had accepted an invitation to a party given by a junior executive with a recording company. He was one of the men Jill suspected of involvement in a white-slavery ring. She'd carefully avoided eating or drinking anything at his house. Sure enough, the other women began showing signs of having been drugged.

That had been the most frightening experience of Jill's life. She'd foolishly neglected to tell anyone where she was going; she had tried to call Kent, but his phone was busy and her companions didn't want to wait.

However, she feigned nausea and managed to escape to a bedroom, where she rapidly dialed Kent's number. That time she reached him. He was furious, but he drove out, accompanied by the police. They found enough evidence, including the drugged remains of drinks in the women's glasses, to break up the ring, and Jill had a great scoop.

But things had never been the same with Kent. Instead of taking pleasure in the award she won for her series, he insisted on regarding her success as a direct slap at him for having turned down the idea in the first place. She hadn't given up hoping they'd work things out, until the day it was announced that Kent was leaving to take a newspaper job in Cincinnati. And he hadn't even told her.

Jill shook herself back to the present. She was standing, daydreaming like a schoolgirl.

She hurried out of the conference room, noticing that the clock on the newsroom wall showed it was almost five. Kent was just closing up his office.

"When and where is this party?" she asked.

"It starts at six; it's at a hotel in Anaheim," Kent said.

"Do I need to dress up? I guess I should stop by my apartment and clean up anyway. I haven't even dropped off my stuff."

"Where are you staying?"

She quickly explained that a friend, Lanni Lopez, an art historian, had suggested Jill house-sit her apartment in Buena Park while Lanni spent a month in Europe at a conference. It was good luck for her, Lanni said; she always worried about burglars. This way, Jill could stay nearby and run up to her own apartment in West Los Angeles, forty-five minutes or so away, once or twice a week if she needed anything.

"I'll tell you what," Kent said. "Why don't you give me the address and I'll pick you up in about an hour and a half? I'd like to run by my place, too, and we don't have to be there the minute the thing starts."

"Okay." She wrote the address down on a slip of paper. "Hey, look, I hope we're not going to be at each other's throat all night. How about declaring a truce?"

He smiled boyishly. "I'd like that. After a hard week at the paper, I'm ready to cut loose."

Jill headed out the front of the building, collecting her marked-up papers from Cindy, along with copies of the day's home and street editions.

She was about to turn away when she was struck by the way Cindy kept her head averted. A second look told Jill the younger woman had been crying.

Despite her own keyed-up feeling, an instinctive wave of sympathy wouldn't let her simply walk away and ignore the situation.

"You know, you could really be a big help to me while I'm here, Cindy," Jill said.

"Oh?" The secretary still wouldn't meet her eyes.

"Everybody else here is so wrapped up in their work—and has so much at stake—they don't have time to fill me in on little things," Jill explained, improvising as she went.

"Like what?" Cindy's curiosity appeared to be getting the better of her.

"Problems people might not think of—anything from stationery supplies coming in late, to inadequate rest-room facilities, to a need for more staff parties," Jill told her. "All those things can have an effect on morale."

"I—I don't think you'd better count on me for much," Cindy replied in a muffled voice, addressing the floor. "I have a feeling I'm not going to be around much longer."

When some rustling sounds came from the publisher's office, Cindy clamped her mouth shut. Clearly she didn't feel comfortable talking around here.

"I was thinking of getting some coffee at a snack shop I saw down the street, and I hate to drink alone," Jill said. "Any chance I could persuade you to join me?"

The younger woman finally looked up. "You'd really like to have coffee with me?" Her amazement, as if she were being singled out for some great honor, made Jill feel slightly embarrassed.

"Look, I may be the consultant, but I'm not all that much older than you, and I'm coming into a new situation where a lot of people are going to be wary of me," she said. "I could use a friend."

"Sure." Cindy's expression brightened. "I was about to leave for the day anyway. Maybe I better check with my boss before I go though," she added as an afterthought.

A check in his office apparently produced no complications, and in a moment the two young women were swinging out the door together.

As she tucked her briefcase and papers into the Dart and drove to meet Cindy, Jill reflected that it would have been nice to have the extra time to loll in the bath before Kent arrived. But she'd have plenty of chances to do that over the weekend; right now, she sensed a fellow human being in need. Besides, she couldn't help liking Cindy.

The two found a booth in the almost-empty snack shop and ordered coffee.

"This must all seem kind of small town to you after Los Angeles," Cindy said as they waited for their order.

Jill shook her head. "Hardly. Newspapers like the *Journal* are the backbone of the business. One thing I've learned is that you can find outstanding work in some of the most out-of-the-way places, and some very poor decisions at major papers. I can learn a lot from some 'small-town' editors."

The coffee arrived, and she decided to tackle the subject head-on. "What did you mean about not being around much longer?" Jill asked.

Cindy's mouth tightened as she stirred two packets of sugar into her cup, and Jill hoped she wasn't going to start crying again. "I guess you heard about this afternoon."

"Mmm." Jill waited.

"I'm really a klutz, aren't I?" Cindy blurted out. "Who ever heard of a secretary dropping her sandwich on the floor and sending her boss into a skid?"

Jill chuckled. "I like the way you phrased that."

"I guess it does sound kind of funny, but it doesn't feel that way." The secretary's shoulders drooped. "I'm surprised Arnold hasn't fired me already. Maybe I'm the comic relief."

"You do have secretarial skills, don't you?" Jill asked. "Typing and all that?"

"Oh, sure," Cindy said. "But nobody ever taught me there was more to being a secretary than taking dictation and answering the phone and filing. There's a lot more, and I don't know how to get a hold on it. Real secretaries are always organized and smooth and practically perfect, and I'm a mess."

"Don't be so hard on yourself," Jill said, considering how to respond. "Everybody has to learn."

"But everything I do is wrong!" Cindy wailed. "I fumble, I look like a kid, I say the wrong things. It's hopeless! I might as well resign before I get the ax."

"Nonsense." Jill sipped at her coffee and leaned back. "I'd say the fact that you want to improve is a very good indication. It must be hard to make the transition from student to professional woman, but I have a feeling you're going to succeed."

The younger woman looked up dubiously, her sorrowful expression and big eyes giving the impression of a small child hoping someone will magically heal her hurts. "What can I do?"

"This is one case where it's probably easier to work from the outside in," Jill said. "Start by looking at the image you present—your clothes, your desk, all the external stuff. Find somebody you think would be a good role model, and try to follow her example."

Cindy considered for a moment and then her expression cheered. "Okay! I know just the person, too! But...do you really think it'll turn me into Priscilla Perfect?"

Jill grinned. "I hate to cramp the style of someone original enough to undo a publisher with a mere tuna sandwich. I think you'll always be Cindy, but you can bring out the parts of her that make a good secretary."

"Thanks. I'll do my best, I really will!"

A few minutes later, Jill was on her way. It did seem unlikely, on the surface, that the helter-skelter secretary could turn herself into a model of cool efficiency, but then, a newspaper wasn't a law firm, either. If Cindy were willing to work at it, she should be able to shape up as much as she needed to.

It felt good to see someone trying to pull herself together instead of just drifting along, Jill reflected as she drove. *I guess that was never my problem though.*

Kent was right about one thing: Jill had always been ambitious, although not in the cold-blooded sense he implied. She hadn't dated much in high school and college, and after Kent left, she'd been too crushed to get involved with anyone for a long time. Then she'd discovered that most of the men she met either wanted her to put her career second to their slightest whim or were willing to accept her career because they themselves didn't want to get too intimately involved in a relationship.

Jill put these thoughts into perspective during the short ride to her temporary new home.

Lanni's apartment was only a half-mile away in an attractive small complex with wooden decks and lots of landscaping. There was a Jacuzzi whirlpool bath and a small swimming pool, Jill noted as she lugged her suitcase through the central courtyard and up a flight of steps to the second floor.

The apartment was light and cheerful, with a large living room opening onto a private balcony and decorated in earth tones with a colorful serape splashed on the wall. There was a sparkling-clean kitchen, a small bedroom, and a bathroom with a separate foyer-dressing room that contained a double closet with sliding mirrored doors.

Setting her suitcase on the bed, Jill realized she'd needed a break from her routine. Although she liked her own apartment, she'd spent too much time working out of it, consulting with a number of small papers around the Los Angeles area, mostly on changing a single section of the paper or one aspect, such as the typefaces and logos.

She had come to California at the invitation of an old newspaper colleague who headed the Newspaper Design Center. Although the work itself sounded exciting, Jill's main motivation had been change.

In her early twenties, getting ahead as a newspaperwoman had seemed an endlessly challenging task. It had enabled her to bury the pain of losing Kent; she'd poured all her energy into reporting and, later, editing, moving to larger papers as opportunities presented themselves. But about a year before, when she was twenty-eight, she'd begun to feel restless and dissatisfied. She was respected in her field, but Jill wanted more than that from life. So she'd moved west in the hope of finding the nameless thing she sought.

Certainly the change had been diverting at first. She'd made some friends and spent her weekends exploring the sights of Southern California, from Malibu to Catalina Island to Mission San Juan Capistrano. Yet after a while the novelty faded, and her half-hearted stabs at free-lance writing hadn't satisfied her either.

Meeting Kent again had been difficult, as she'd anticipated ever since seeing his name on the editorial page of the *Journal* and realizing she'd have to work with him. But she hadn't expected the cluster of mixed emotions, the stab of longing, and the rush of physical pleasure whenever he touched her.

And it was all useless. No matter how she felt, no matter how much they might still have in common, it was clear she'd turned out to be the wrong woman for him. And Anita made it perfectly clear that there were plenty of other women ready to bat their eyelashes and mold themselves into whatever Kent wanted. Sometimes Jill almost wished she could be like that. *No!* She told herself firmly, shaking out a slightly wrinkled dress. *Any man I fall in love with has got to want me for myself.*

Jill hesitated over which dress to wear. It was a Halloween party, so perhaps she should aim for some unusual effect, but on the other hand, she didn't want the staff to get a first impression of her as some kind of kook. She settled on a summery tan silk dress with a flattering low V neck, a high waistline, and unusual sleeves gathered at the wrist but slit all the way up to the shoulder. People would just have to understand that she hadn't been prepared to come in costume.

Kent arrived promptly at six. She jumped at the sound of his knock, reproaching herself for the sudden surge of nervousness. Opening the door, Jill found herself momentarily speechless. He'd changed from his slightly askew business suit to a casual maroon shirt, open at the throat, and tailored gray slacks. He looked startlingly handsome and touchable.

"I like that dress," he said, his eyes glinting warmly. "For a dragon lady, you sure hide it well. Maybe that's a poor choice of words; that dress doesn't hide much of anything."

"Do you think it's too revealing?" she asked worriedly.

He laughed. "Hardly. It's just that a man can't help noticing certain things. Don't worry about it. At least there's two of us who aren't dressed up as anything."

Kent escorted her down to his silver Mercedes. "Pretty snappy for an editor," she teased as she slid inside.

He walked around and entered on the driver's side. "As you may have forgotten, my family is from Orange County and my grandparents made some good investments in real estate. Then the boom came along and put us all in good shape."

"You don't have to work then," she observed.

"Not true," he said. "It takes money to keep up real estate, and I'd rather not sell anything off until I really need it. Besides, what else would I do? Even if you could afford not to, wouldn't you work?"

"I don't know," Jill said. "I suppose I would, but I'd take some time off. Travel, see Europe and the Orient."

"Hmm." He glanced over and let his eyes linger for a moment on her figure. "Maybe it would be more accurate to say you'd let Europe and the Orient see you."

She felt a tingling in her breasts and a headiness, as if she'd drunk too much champagne. "I've never really let go," she joked. "It might be fun, nude sunbathing at Saint-Tropez or on a yacht off Monte Carlo."

"Promise you'll send pictures?" He chuckled again and she laughed with him.

"You know I'm much too modest," she sighed. "How about you, Kent? Isn't there something you'd like to do after all these years of deadlines and kid reporters who have to be whipped into shape?"

"To tell the truth..." He stopped speaking to concentrate as he turned up a freeway on ramp and merged into the heavy Friday rush-hour traffic. "I know what I want, but I haven't found it yet."

"What's that?"

"I'm not about to tell anyone."

"That's not fair. I told you my daydreams."

"This isn't a daydream," he said seriously. She felt oddly disappointed, even a little hurt, at being left out of his confidence. Once she had known everything he thought, or so she'd imagined.

Afterward, she could never remember which hotel they went to, except that it was many-storied with an elegant lobby and lots of people scurrying around. Anaheim, home of Disneyland, the California Angels baseball team, and the Los Angeles Rams football players, was a city populated largely by giant hotels. The Press Club had been accorded a large, red-carpeted ballroom and a long buffet table with a swan ice sculpture in the center. Winging out on either side of the sculpture were luscious bowls of chilled shrimp, fruit-studded Styrofoam towers, fans of crackers and cheeses, and chafing dishes full of spicy meatballs and Chinese spareribs.

The room was already crammed with costumed members of the press. Jill spotted a pair of Star Trekkies and a Darth Vader, two short women disguised as a pair of dice in paper-covered boxes marked with black construction-paper dots, a couple in pioneer dress, a man wrapped in yards of old recording tape—he claimed he was the Watergate tapes—and dozens of others.

They had just reached the bar when Anita Ruiz sidled up. She looked exotically seductive in a harem dancer outfit with a skimpy halter top and puffy gauze pants gathered at the ankles. Her dark hair fell loosely over her shoulders, and her eyes swam mysteriously amid swirls of eyeliner.

"Kent!" Anita cried in welcome. "Haven't we got a great turnout? I'm so glad you could come."

"What, me miss a Press Club party?" he teased. "You know you'd have to tie me to a printing press to keep me away."

Anita favored Jill with a cold look. "I'm sure our new consultant will want to meet everybody. Come on, honey, I'll introduce you to some of the reporters..."

"Not so fast, Anita," Kent said. "Jill and I have a few things to discuss."

She pouted. "You're not going to talk about business at my party, are you? Anyway, we need Jill to help judge some of the costume contests. It's hard to find people who can be objective."

Jill and Kent exchanged slightly exasperated glances. It was hard to refuse Anita without being rude or making it appear they were attached to each other by more than professional concerns. Grudgingly Kent conceded. Jill would have liked to think he held back because he enjoyed her company, but she suspected it was more because he didn't want Anita buzzing over him all night.

The features editor whisked Jill to the opposite side of the room and presented her to a small knot of people who had also been asked to judge. They came from a variety of tabloids around the county, and she distracted herself from her disappointment by using the opportunity to learn more about their papers.

After a while she glanced over and saw Kent talking to Anita, who had placed her hand possessively on his arm. Halfway into a drink, the managing editor appeared to have relaxed, and the scantily clad presence of an apparently willing harem dancer was taking away the rest of his reserve.

Then he glanced up at Jill and his gaze traveled to the two people standing with her, the middle-aged editor of a small but growing paper in the south county and the publisher of the *Journal*'s main opposition. His expression hardened and he turned away.

Blast him anyway! Jill thought, accepting a glass of wine from a passing waitress. *Does he always have to draw the wrong conclusion about everything I do?*

Raffle tickets were sold for a scholarship fund, and then the contests began. Some of the categories were standard—most unusual costume, most authentic costume—and then there were such designations as costume that best represented the history of Orange County. It went to a woman who'd come dressed as an orange crate, plastered with colorful pictures of Mexican maidens holding baskets of brightly colored fruit.

At last the judging ended and the raffle began. Feeling displaced, Jill looked around for Kent. He was standing with Anita and three other people in one corner, laughing and quite evidently enjoying himself.

Jill was just debating whether to take a cab home when Arnold caught her eye.

"You look lost," he said. "I'm surprised at seeing so attractive a lady without a flock of men around her."

"Thanks." She blushed at the compliment. "Actually I'm glad I was able to help judge. I've met so many people today I can't keep them all straight, and I know at these gatherings everyone likes to cut loose with their friends, not make polite talk with a consultant."

"I'd like to think you are one of my friends," Arnold said. "Frankly it's hard for me to relax with the staff from the *Journal*. I don't believe we're really on opposite sides, but I am kind of a stranger here myself."

Jill was grateful to have someone she could converse with comfortably. She knew she had to be careful in some areas; after all, Arnold was still in a sense her boss, and she didn't want to give him a bad impression. However, he seemed inclined to think well of her and, as he had said, they both had a common goal for the *Journal*.

They were just discussing some recent news about an expansion at a major Los Angeles paper when Jill realized Kent was at her elbow.

"Oh, hi," she said.

"Remember me?" His satiric words had an angry edge to them, which she chose to ignore.

"I didn't want to interrupt your conversation," she said. "Besides, Arnold is here by himself."

"If you're tied up, I'd be happy to give Jill a ride home," Arnold said. "That is, assuming she didn't bring her own car."

Jill waited for Kent to respond. Maybe it would be better if they weren't alone together again; judging by his expression, she had a feeling that all they would do was fight.

Kent seemed to be forcing a polite tone into his words to his boss. "It might look better to the staff if we spread her around a little. I don't mind taking her home. As you've said in the past, Arnold, we want everyone to see we're on the same side. You did say that, didn't you?"

Arnold's jaw tightened at the challenge in the words, and Jill wondered again why the two were so hostile to each other. But all the publisher said was, "I'm glad you're coming to realize that. We are all in this together, you and me and Jill. Whatever we may say in private, I think it's best if we present a united front in public."

Jill glanced up and saw Anita jiggling toward them. "Speaking of a united front," she murmured. Her jest broke the tension, and the two men chuckled.

"Oh, Kent!" Anita said with forced cheerfulness. "I was wondering where you'd wandered off to! Isn't it lucky Mr. Latimore's here? I'm sure he'd be happy to take Jill home."

"We've already been through that," Kent said. "It seems his wife is insanely jealous."

"Since when?" Anita stopped herself and shrugged. "Oh, well. See you Monday, then."

Jill was glad when they stepped back out into the clear autumn night. The temperature was dropping rapidly and she shivered. To her surprise, Kent put his arm around her.

"If I had a jacket, I'd give it to you, but I'm afraid I forgot to plan ahead myself," he said as they hurried to the car. Jill, enjoying the warmth of his touch, wished he wouldn't make it sound so much like a duty.

As they drove slowly back toward her apartment, the faint masculine scent of him and the angle of his face as he watched the road ahead took her back to Nashville. She could almost imagine they were going home together as they had all those years ago. The memory brought with it a bittersweet pain, and she wondered if he were thinking the same thing.

Kent parked the car without a word and they walked side by side up the steps, each lost in private thoughts. At the top he waited while Jill fumbled with the unfamiliar key and opened the door.

"Would you like some coffee?" she asked. "Or a drink? I think I saw a bottle of Scotch around here somewhere."

Kent shook his head. "Actually, it's been a long day—for both of us, I imagine."

He hesitated, and Jill waited until he spoke again.

"We didn't get much chance to talk tonight," Kent said. "Things will be pretty hectic Monday—not the best time to discuss things calmly. If you don't have other plans, I'll pick you up for dinner tomorrow night about seven."

The suddenness of his suggestion caught Jill off guard. "Sure," she answered, then shivered as a wind smelling of salt water chilled by her.

Kent's hands rubbed gently up her arms, prickling them with warmth. Standing so close to him, Jill felt small, vulnerable... and protected.

As if it were the most natural thing in the world, he bent down, his mouth finding hers with tender thoroughness. The kiss emptied her and filled her up again, as though her heart had leaped for one suspended moment into his body and then had come back again, bringing his with it.

"Kent," Jill whispered, staring up at him with astonishment when he drew back. "I..."

He blinked sharply, as if awakening, then released her abruptly. "Tomorrow night then." He turned away and hurried down the steps.

The night was a restless one for Jill, alone in a strange bed, acutely sensitive to every sound—the distant barking of a dog, the murmur of an occasional car on the street.

Kent's nearness still sparked electricity between them, as it always had, she realized as she lay remembering their unexpected moment together.

She wasn't sure whether she had been afraid of that, of the renewal of their mutual attraction despite the knowledge that they were totally unsuitable, or whether she had been more afraid that she would see him and feel nothing at all. In a way that would have been a kind of death, she perceived, the death of the only real passion she had ever felt for a man.

But it was all so hopeless. And so were her attempts to sleep, until the early morning hours when exhaustion finally claimed her.

Jill slept late, then spent the day exploring the apartment and the neighborhood, a quiet area with a convenient grocery store and pharmacy and not much else. Returning home, she thought about her outfit for the evening. She decided on a soft, ruffled turquoise blouse and a black skirt as suitably dressy yet businesslike.

Kent arrived punctually, his expression impersonal as he greeted her and escorted her to the car. Despite the smoothness of his manner, she noted a tension about his face and shoulders and wondered if he was regretting having invited her.

A valet helped her out at the restaurant, an elegant, modern establishment that featured steak and lobster. Kent laid his arm on her waist as they walked toward the building, his touch arousing a disquieting sense of longing.

They were given a corner booth, complete with romantic candlelight. Kent ordered wine and they kept their conversation light until they had selected their dinners.

Finally the waiter left and Jill looked over at Kent uncertainly. "I suppose it seems like I'm barging back into your life in a rather awkward way," she said. "Coming in and working for the new owners, I mean."

He studied her expressionlessly. "You have a job to do. If you can do it objectively, we shouldn't have any difficulties."

"And what makes you think I won't be objective?" she challenged.

He shrugged. "You're in a very political situation. There are a lot of opportunities here to get ahead, make the right impression with the right people."

"Oh, really!" Jill snapped. "I think you're blowing this out of proportion."

The waiter set spinach salads in front of them, and their talk was suspended until he ground the pepper and departed.

"I couldn't help noticing last night that you gravitate to the top," Kent said, taking a sip of his wine. "That was some company you were keeping. I guess you picked up quite a bit of information that could be useful in your business. Maybe even heard of some job openings."

"You're beginning to sound like a stuck record," Jill said. "If you don't cut it out, I'm going to toss this salad right in your lap."

Kent grinned. "You're right. I've been pushing you rather hard, haven't I?"

He reached out and cupped his hand over hers, and Jill forgot what she wanted to say next. She toyed with her water glass before meeting his gaze again. "Kent, I wish we could get the past out of the way. It's obvious we both got hurt. Neither one of us did it deliberately."

"To tell the truth, I've been a little surprised at myself," Kent said. "I always imagined that if we met again, I'd feel nothing but indifference."

"That's not flattering." She watched the candleglow trace the outline of his cheekbones.

"I remembered you as a feisty little reporter trying to get ahead. You've turned into a rather complex woman," he said.

The waiter arrived with their main course—steak for him, shrimp in garlic sauce for her. Jill savored the delicious meal for a few minutes before picking up the conversation again.

"Can't we start from scratch, Kent?" she said. "We respect each other's abilities, at least I think we do, and that's a good basis for a professional relationship."

"A professional relationship," he repeated. "That has a nice ring to it. Do they teach you phrases like that at management seminars?"

Impulsively she dipped a finger into her water glass and flicked some liquid at him. The drop of water caught him square in the nose and he snorted in surprise.

"Any other smart cracks you want to make?" she asked sweetly, hand poised near the glass.

He dried his face with a napkin. "If we weren't in polite society, I'd teach you a thing or two about water fights."

"Oh, yeah?" she said. "Well, it just so happens

there's both a whirlpool and a swimming pool at my apartment house, so if you'd like me to take you up on that, I will."

Kent nodded in self-satisfaction. "Since like a true native Californian I always carry a swimsuit in the trunk of my car, I accept your challenge."

As she unlocked the door to the apartment, Jill was beginning to wonder if it was such a good idea. They had dated for a long time in Nashville before becoming lovers, but when they had, their passion had been explosive.

She'd never wanted another man the same way since then and knew that such close contact in a state of semi-undress could be dangerous. Yet one glance at Kent's broad chest and equally broad smile as he headed for the bathroom to change into his swimsuit and she knew she couldn't back down.

She changed in the bedroom, picking a delicate French bikini in a pure white that emphasized her own tan. Slipping on thong sandals, Jill stepped out and took an admiring look at Kent in his sky-blue trunks. His body was impressive, strong, and firm, but what drew her most was his restless energy, the feeling of bottled-up masculinity that could explode at any moment.

Kent let out a low whistle. "If insulting you in a restaurant gets me this, I'll have to think of lots of nasty things to say."

Jill hesitated. "Kent, you know we're playing with fire."

"Then let's put it out...in the swimming pool." He grabbed her hand and they ran outside.

The air was cool but the water was heated, a fact she discovered as Kent caught her off guard with a shove that splashed her into the middle of the water. Fortunately there was no one else around to be inconvenienced by their horseplay.

He dove in beside her, and Jill realized right away she was overmatched physically. If she stayed where she was, he could dunk her at will.

Instead she swam toward a corner of the pool where several beach balls were floating, with the vague idea of lobbing one of them at him. But her eyes fell on something even better, a child's water pistol, carelessly left on the concrete edge of the pool. Keeping her body between it and Kent so he couldn't see, she slid the weapon into the water and withdrew the plug, hearing a faint glug of bubbles as it filled up.

"What are you doing over there?" Kent approached, a smug look on his face. Despite the bright overhead lights, Jill was thankful for the shadows that hid her secret. "Don't tell me you've given up that easily."

"Why don't you come over here and find out?" she dared him.

"You're up to something, aren't you? Well, so am I." He reached out to grab her, but she moved too quickly, whipping around and blasting him in the face with a spray of water.

"Ach!" He stumbled back, sneezing.

"How do you like them apples, tough guy?" she chortled, refilling the water pistol.

Kent shook his head, laughing ruefully. "Where'd you get that blasted thing? Well, here's a little trick I learned as a kid." He made a wedge with his hands and sent a shower in her direction. She fired back, but soon ran out of water, and he seized the opportunity to lunge toward her.

They wrestled out into the deep water, giggling and gasping as they struggled. In his strong grasp Jill found herself easily manipulated, although Kent was careful never to keep her under for more than a few seconds. Her struggles only served to entangle them more closely, his bare legs twining around hers to keep her from kicking.

Finally, exhausted, she stopped fighting and found herself lifted in his arms. Her hands circled his neck as if of their own will, and he bent over her, pressing his lips to hers. Gently, but with an underlying fierceness that wiped away any thought of opposition, he explored her mouth, tasting the sweetness within.

"Kent," she whispered.

Slowly he lowered her until she stood on the bottom of the pool, feeling the water lap around her shoulders as he took her hand and led her out.

Both shivered, and Jill realized she'd forgotten to bring towels.

With one thought they climbed down into the whirlpool bath, savoring the hot water. Kent flipped a switch and jets swirled the heat around them, the sound and faint spray drowning out the rest of the world.

He sat on the underwater bench and pulled her onto his lap, her wet hair curtaining them as they nuzzled each other. The rough skin of his cheeks excited her as he traced his lips over her throat and down toward the valley between her breasts. Jill leaned back and felt one strap slip off her shoulder.

Through the spray of water, Kent's mouth found her nipple, and she gasped involuntarily as his tongue traced the brown tip. Longing throbbed through her, and it was only with an effort that she remembered they were out of doors and might be seen.

"Maybe we should go inside," she murmured, and he nodded, reluctantly sitting up and helping her pull her bikini top back into place.

After switching off the rushing jets, they climbed the stairs hand in hand, leaving little puddles behind them. Once inside, they hurried across the carpet into the bathroom, where they toweled each other playfully. When the straps to her top slipped down again, Jill felt Kent, his arms around her, tug gently at the knotted back and the bikini top fell to the floor.

He stepped back to admire her, his hands moving up from her waist to massage the taut peaks. Jill moaned, her whole body aching for him, the intensifying pressure on her nipples obliterating everything else from her mind.

Kent leaned over her again, kissing her hungrily, licking at the inside of her mouth as she responded eagerly. His bare chest pressed against her swollen breasts, further enflaming her. She stroked his back, feeling the muscular shoulders as he pulled her closer against him.

Seizing a fresh towel, he drew her into the bedroom and spread the dry terry cloth beneath them as they sat, unable to tear themselves apart for even a moment. His hands caressed her shoulders, her back, the inward curve of her stomach and the soft, vulnerable warmth below. Jill lowered her cheek against his shoulder.

Firmly Kent eased her onto the bed, and she felt his hands tug at the elastic on her bikini bottoms. In a moment he lay beside her, bare skin pressing together along their bodies. He was ready for her, but he took his time, kissing, sucking at her nipples, rousing her to desire she had never experienced before.

"Jill," he whispered tenderly. "Oh, Jill, you're so beautiful. I tried to forget but I couldn't." She silenced him with a kiss, ardent and provocative, until he could wait no longer. She felt him climb on top of her and then cried out softly.

Fire mounted inside her as he pressed deeper and deeper, still caressing her breasts, seeking her mouth and probing it lovingly. Great flames licked through her; she heard his answering groan, and then they lay quiet in the afterglow.

Chapter Three

Kent had to leave early the next morning to drive to Palm Springs for his aunt and uncle's anniversary celebration. Feeling restless, Jill walked down to the corner convenience store to pick up several newspapers.

As she walked back to her apartment, the papers tucked under her arm, she tried to sort out her thoughts about Kent. He'd been so loving last night and this morning, it was as if everything had been washed clean between them. Yet nothing was really resolved.

They were still the same people they'd always been. In his arms she found herself yielding, but in everyday life she was still independent, career-minded Jill, and he had shown before that wasn't what he liked in a woman.

The minute she entered her living room and opened the *Journal*'s competitor, she knew there was going to be trouble.

Splashed across the front page was a feature on the Siamese twins. To make matters worse, the story indicated the interview had been conducted on Saturday.

It was all Anita's fault, but that wasn't going to help. Jill remembered Arnold saying that the condition of sale was that he couldn't fire anyone without cause. Surely being scooped on one story wasn't enough for Kent to lose his job, but it had been his decision to wait until Monday. Still, she had agreed with his reasoning, but had Arnold?

Kent didn't call that night, and she realized she didn't have his home phone number, although he'd carefully written hers down before leaving. Perhaps he didn't get home until late and didn't want to risk waking her, she told herself. Surely even if he'd seen the newspaper, he couldn't blame her for it.

Jill purposely spent Monday morning at her apartment, marking up the Sunday *Journal*. The staff of the paper would be on deadline, and probably tension was running high. There was no point in making the situation worse.

She couldn't stay away all day, however, and Arnold had specifically mentioned wanting to see her, so about eleven o'clock Jill nosed her Dart into the parking lot of the *Journal*.

Cindy looked up cheerfully as she walked in. Her blond hair had been cut in a wedge that was both neat and flattering.

"You look great," Jill said. "I didn't expect such a big change so soon."

Cindy basked in the praise. "I just couldn't wait," she said. "I'm afraid I won't be able to buy any new clothes until my next paycheck, but I wanted to make a noticeable start."

Jill glanced at the mottoes and troll dolls on the desk. "Mmm, you might want to do something about those," she suggested as tactfully as she could.

Cindy followed her gaze, then looked up, startled. "I never noticed before, but you're right. That doesn't look good for someone walking into the publisher's office, does it?"

"Speaking of which, is he in?" Jill asked. "He mentioned wanting to talk to me today."

"Of course!" Cindy knocked at the office door, then ushered Jill inside. She offered to fix coffee without waiting for Arnold to ask, and both women were pleased by the look of surprise on his face. However, both Jill and Arnold declined, since it was nearly lunchtime.

"You know, I think she's finally coming around," Arnold said as Jill settled down. "That haircut is a vast improvement."

"She's really making an effort," Jill said. "I'm pleased, because she seems like a nice person."

"Yes, of course." Arnold dismissed the subject. "I don't want to take too much of your time. I guess you saw yesterday's papers?"

Jill nodded.

"What was your professional opinion?"

"I think we got scooped."

He smiled. "I'd say so." Then the expression faded. "But this isn't the first time, although it's the most flagrant example."

"What do you mean?" Jill leaned forward, curious.

"It's embarrassing. A couple of weeks ago one of our police reporters spent several days working up a feature on a new program in which troubled youngsters were being paired with police officers, kind of a variation of Big Brothers," Arnold said. "I don't have to tell you, this isn't the kind of paper that can afford to put reporters on stories for any length of time, but Kent felt there was a lot of interest, and I didn't disagree with that."

"And you got scooped?"

Arnold nodded. "Oh, I'll admit their story wasn't as good as ours. Their reporter just interviewed a couple of people in one afternoon. But when we came out with our story after they'd run theirs, it looked as if we were playing monkey-see monkey-do."

"That can happen to any newspaper," Jill said. "I don't expect there's so much happening around here that two reporters wouldn't stumble on things at the same time once in a while."

"That's true," Arnold said. "But if things don't sharpen up around here, we're going to be in real trouble when we launch our campaign. The owners are putting a lot of money into this and it could get ugly. Have you ever been in the middle of a newspaper war, Jill?"

She shook her head. "They're not too common these days."

"I go back a little before your time." Arnold frowned, and Jill noticed that his hands were clenched in fists. "The bigger paper has a lot of advantages. It can offer cut rates on ads—give them away, if it wants to—launch some really expensive promotions, even revamp its own format if it decides that's necessary. And it's got the edge: the subscribers and the advertisers."

"It sounds risky," Jill said.

He nodded. "Coastal Communications Group could lose a bundle. But we feel Orange County is growing enough to be worth it, and there are a lot of needs we think aren't being met. The problem is, we've got to offer the readers something they can't get anywhere else, and if the opposition is consistently beating us to the punch, we can't do that."

"I see what you mean," Jill said. "But I know Kent is an excellent editor. I really don't think this kind of thing is likely to keep happening."

"Let me warn you about something, Jill," Arnold said. "I noticed our handsome bachelor managing editor was giving you something of a rush Friday night. There are some things you might not have known about him when you were just a reporter, or maybe he's changed."

"Like what?"

"He's rather unscrupulous where women are concerned," Arnold said. "And you're a particularly inviting target."

"Somehow that doesn't sound like you're flattering me," Jill said.

"I wasn't referring to your obviously attractive appearance," Arnold said, his tone warming for a moment. "I'm afraid, as you may have observed, that Kent and I haven't hit it off too well."

"I can see that your approach to newspapering is a little different," she conceded.

"It goes beyond that," Arnold said. "It's a power struggle, as you've probably gathered. I represent CCG, but I'm not the owner, the way Michael was. I'm responsible to somebody else for what happens to this paper, just as he's responsible to me. So I've got something to prove, too."

"I still don't see what that has to do with me."

"You're independent," Arnold said. "I didn't hire you; CCG did, although I happen to agree with their decision. Kent knows his job is on the line if he botches up, so it's certainly to his advantage to win you to his side. I've watched him around women enough to know that he can be a real charmer when he wants to, and I suspect he's been giving you a pretty heavy dose. I wouldn't like to see you be used, Jill."

She felt a cold lump in the pit of her stomach and tried to argue it away. Kent was nothing if not honest; she couldn't imagine his seducing her, pretending to care about her, just so he could keep his job. But at the same time it was hard to explain his inviting her to go to the party with him and the way he'd seemed to alternate between sarcasm and flirtation.

"Thanks for the warning," she said. "Was there anything else you wanted to see me about?"

Arnold shook his head. "Not yet. I think I'd better give you time to look around a bit more before we talk over any changes we're going to make."

Jill stepped out and hesitated. She wanted to let Cindy know that Arnold had noticed the change in her, but the secretary was chattering away into the phone on what was obviously a private conversation.

Then Cindy noticed her and quickly brought the chat to an end. "I'm sorry," she said, hanging up the phone. "I didn't see you there."

Jill bent over and said in a low voice, "I just wanted to let you know Arnold commented favorably on the change in you. I think you've made a good start."

"Oh, thanks!" Cindy sat up straighter. "If you have any other suggestions, please don't hold back."

"Well, actually," Jill said, "I don't want to

seem too critical, but it isn't a good idea to have long personal conversations while you're working."

Cindy's face fell. "That was just Tim, my boyfriend. We do tend to talk a lot, I guess. Mr. Latimore never seems to mind. Tim is interested in newspapers, too, so we have a lot to chat about, but you're right. I'll try to wait until I get home."

"I know it isn't easy, but you're doing great," Jill added, sensing the younger woman needed more encouragement, and was rewarded with a smile.

She didn't feel so cheerful herself as she made her way back to the newsroom. It was much fuller than on Friday afternoon; reporters were finishing up their work before lunch, although the eleven-thirty deadline had already passed.

Work was really just getting into full swing for the copydesk, though. Jill didn't see Kent around, so she stopped by Lewis France's desk. He gave her a cordial nod, so she watched as he edited a story on the screen, moving blocks of copy around with a few pushes of a button.

Once the copy was written, it still had to be edited, and then the pages had to be laid out and the headlines created. The process had been greatly simplified since the days before computers—only a few years ago—but copydeskers still had to possess very quick minds, an excellent command of English and of newspaper style, and the experience to whip out accurate headlines that fit in the space allotted. Writing headlines was one of the hardest tasks there was on a newspaper, Jill reflected wryly.

She was beginning to feel comfortable, as the copy editors clearly didn't mind her observing, until she heard footsteps and looked up to see Kent glaring at her. He jerked his head in the direction of his office, and although she resented his abruptness, she decided it was better to cooperate than to risk an argument in front of the staff.

He didn't mince words. As soon as she closed the door behind her, Kent snapped, "I don't suppose you have an explanation for this?" and held up the article about the twins.

"Me?" Jill said, caught off guard. "For heaven's sake, Kent, you're not making sense."

"Oh, I'm not, am I?" He paced around the small office like a caged lion. "Do you think I didn't see whom you were talking with at the Press Club party?"

"You mean Arnold?" she asked, confused.

"Oh, for heaven's sake, don't play innocent with me!" His blue eyes darkened with anger. "I'm talking about the publisher of a certain newspaper we both know about."

Then Jill remembered standing with the publisher of the opposition paper, but the implication dumbfounded her. Finally her voice came out in a squeak. "Are you trying to say you think I leaked word of this story? Kent, that's crazy!"

"Is it?" He seemed calmer, but his fury was only better controlled, not abated. "I can think of several ways you could get a top position at a good newspaper, and this looks like one of them."

Tears burned just beneath the surface. She couldn't understand why he was willfully misunderstanding her, accusing her of trying to sabotage him for her own gain.

Mistaking her silence for stubbornness, he went on, "Are you pretending you wouldn't like to get in the publisher's good graces? Our rival is a big paper, and they pay well."

"That's not fair!"

"Or maybe you'd like my job," he pushed on relentlessly. "You've probably guessed by now the publisher isn't crazy about me. He wants our advertisers to influence our news judgment. Only last week he asked me to downplay a consumer fraud charge against a store, and I refused. He's looking for a rope to hang me with. If we get scooped like this a few more times, Arnold's going to get me fired, and he likes your style—slick and commercial, just like his."

Jill opened her mouth to argue and then closed it again. What was the use? He obviously was going to think the worst of her no matter what happened. Their lovemaking had been an accident, a spur-of-the-moment thing fueled by a few drinks and the usual end-of-the-week release of tension. She refused to believe that Kent had intentionally used her; if he had, he wouldn't lash out at her this way and spoil it all. But his lack of trust was clear evidence that what had happened between them meant nothing to him.

"I've got work to do," she said as coldly as she could, hoping he didn't notice the slight quaver in her voice. "If you need anything, I believe I'll start with the sports section."

She rose and walked out, forcing herself not to look at him. Jill stopped by the ladies' room and locked herself in a stall, where she allowed herself to give vent to tears.

Blast him anyway! What did he mean, coming back into her life, sweeping her off her feet, acting as if he cared about her? She'd been a fool, and worse than that, she'd let her feelings interfere with her work. Now she was going to have to pretend that nothing had happened or else withdraw from the assignment.

She couldn't do that; what explanation would she give? Besides, this had been an important job, one that showed high regard for her abilities. She couldn't let the design center down, and she couldn't let herself down either.

Jill walked back out and washed her face. As she was reapplying her makeup, Anita walked in.

At first the dark-haired woman appeared to ignore her. Then, apparently changing her mind, she turned and addressed Jill directly.

"That wasn't a very clever thing you did," Anita burst out. "You were trying to make me look bad, weren't you?"

"I don't know what you're talking about." Jill continued putting on lipstick.

"I mean leaking the word about our Siamese twin story," Anita cried. "Kent was mad enough because I sat on it all week. He called me in this morning and chewed me out. That's what you had in mind, didn't you? Well, let me tell you, Miss Newspaper Consultant, whatever it is you want, you're not going to get it."

"What I want," Jill said as steadily as she could, "is for people to stop making ridiculous accusations. I don't know who told the opposition about that story, if anybody did. For all I know it was purely a coincidence. But it wasn't me. And the only other thing I want, Anita, is to do my job to the best of my ability around here and then leave and never see any of you again."

Jill snapped her purse shut and walked out of the ladies' room.

Frank Rickles's warm greeting was a welcome relief. He introduced her to the four sportswriters and discussed his ideas for changing and improving the section. The problem with sports was achieving a balance between local sports and national and international events; there was never enough room in the paper. Using agate type, the tiny six-point type for printing scores, could help spread coverage, but it was hard to read and not very satisfying.

As far as Jill could tell, the content and editing of the sports section was perfectly acceptable. However, she and Frank talked about ways to play photographs more dramatically and use boxes— round-cornered rectangles around short items— to dress up the page.

"I have a personal prejudice against jumps," Jill said. "I think when the reader has to turn to page two or whatever to continue reading, he usually doesn't bother, so the rest of the space is wasted. Studies have shown that about sixty percent of your readers don't make the first jump and ninety percent don't make the second."

Frank counted stories on the front of the sports page and found that five of them were continued. "I guess we could cut that down to one or two," he admitted.

They spent the rest of the day discussing other ideas for the sports section, and Jill made copious notes. She felt better, partly because of Frank's willingness to work with her and partly because at least she was accomplishing something.

After work she and Frank and some of the sportswriters adjourned to Sparky's, the local bar. Every newspaper has its preferred hangout, and this was it for the *Journal*.

The place was half-filled, mostly with people Jill didn't recognize, although some of them Frank pointed out as being from the back shop. The place reminded her of their hangout in Nashville.

"Sometimes I think I'd like to go back to being a reporter," she told Frank.

"You can tell they're getting old when they talk like that," he kidded. "You forget about the late-night city council meetings? How about the cops who give you a hard time?"

"The cops never gave me a hard time."

"I can see why," said one of the writers admiringly, and Jill felt even better.

Then she saw Anita come through the door with Kent right behind her.

"Now there's a sight," said Frank. "She's been after him ever since she got here."

"When was that?" Jill asked.

"Oh, six, eight months ago," he said.

"Somehow I figured she'd been here a long time."

Frank shook his head. "No. Kent hired her just last spring. Her credentials looked pretty good, and who could help noticing what a knockout she is?"

"Boy, it sure didn't take long to figure out she's a stinker though," muttered one of the men, and Jill couldn't help smiling agreement.

"Yeah. I'm surprised to see Kent hanging out with her," said another man.

The conversation quickly steered back onto the upcoming football season, but Jill's thoughts remained with the couple sitting halfway across the room. What was Kent up to anyway? He and Anita weren't being very cuddly, despite her deferential looks and frequent, brittle laugh, but then they'd hardly carry on in front of other staff members.

Gradually Jill's discomfort turned to anger. He'd had no right to accuse her this morning, especially after making love to her only two days before. And even if this meeting with Anita had something to do with business, he was certainly giving everyone else the impression he was interested in her.

Drat him! Jill thought. *I should have learned my lesson the last time.*

She was glad when her companions rose to go home for dinner. She offered to pay the tab, but Frank put on a show of being offended. Jill knew sportswriters tended to be more chauvinistic—or maybe just more chivalrous—than most journalists, so she gracefully accepted his insistence on paying for her glass of wine.

It was still light out, so she declined an offer to accompany her to her car. Anyway, she wanted to go back into the building and fetch her briefcase.

When she came out again, she saw that most of the cars had departed from around the *Journal*, but not the silver Mercedes. Whatever Kent was talking to Anita about, he didn't seem to be in a hurry.

Then Jill saw him walking across the lot toward the car, and she ducked hurriedly into her Dart. Alone, Kent climbed into the Mercedes, and Jill heard the click of a key in the ignition, then nothing.

"Damn!" Kent, the car door still open, continued flicking the ignition on and off, but his battery was clearly dead.

Jill considered leaving him to call the Auto Club by himself, but it occurred to her that driving by without even stopping to offer help would be sinking to his own level of unpleasantness.

She idled her car over. "Something wrong?"

He grimaced. "I got here so early this morning it was still dark, and it looks like I left my lights on."

She pulled her car alongside his and cut her engine. "That's not good for the battery."

"No kidding."

Jill exited her car and opened the trunk.

"Don't tell me you've got jumper cables," Kent said. "You really are the modern woman."

Jill pulled out the cable. "I have to drive a lot on business, and my battery tends to get low on water. I don't like the thought of being stuck out in Modesto or somewhere on a weekend waiting for the Auto Club to show up."

"If you put that thing on backward, it blows up

the engine," Kent observed as she opened the hood of her car and he reluctantly did the same with his.

It was her turn to be sarcastic. "No kidding."

"All right, all right." He watched skeptically as she carefully attached the cables.

"That meet with your approval?" she asked.

He nodded slowly. "Listen, Jill," Kent said, "I've been meaning to tell you I'm sorry I jumped down your throat this morning. I chewed everybody out—I guess you saw me apologizing to Anita."

"Oh, is that what you were doing?" Before he could answer, she added, "Why don't you try to start your car now?"

"Because I want to talk to you first."

She leaned against her car and folded her arms. "Okay, talk."

"You're not making this any easier."

"I'm not trying to. I had a rotten day and furthermore—oh, I don't want to go into it."

"Now you sound like me," he said ruefully. She waited for him to continue, and finally he did. "I've already apologized. I had no business jumping to conclusions like that, but it just seemed to fit . . . well, as you say, let's not get into that."

"I'm surprised you apologized to Anita," she said, the memory of the rest-room conversation still smarting. "After all, she's the one who messed things up in the first place by sitting on a story as good as that one."

"Temper, temper," said Kent.

"You weren't so cool yourself."

"Jill, are you going to accept my apology, or are we going to go on making nasty remarks to each other?"

She stuck out an oil-splashed hand. "Shake."

Kent laughed. "Okay, lady mechanic." He took her hand in a firm grip and shook it, then used his handkerchief to wipe away the oil.

He started his car on the second try, and Jill removed the jumper cables. "You probably know this, but it would be a good idea to drive around for a while to recharge your battery, since you live close by," she said.

He nodded. "Thanks for the reminder."

"Kent," Jill said, "I really am curious. Why did you hire Anita, and why do you keep her on?"

"Seriously?" he said, and she nodded. "Her credentials looked good, and frankly I don't pay too much attention to what goes on in the features section. It's just window-dressing anyway."

"Most readers don't think so," Jill said.

"Let's get one thing straight." Kent leaned out his open door and looked at her seriously. "I know Anita isn't a hard-news reporter or editor like you, but she's a very attractive woman and she's also reasonably good at her job."

"I happen to disagree."

"I didn't expect you to think she was pretty."

Jill remained leaning against her car, unwilling to take the joke. "I meant I think she's the weakest thing at the *Journal*, and I'm going to say so in my report."

"Is that a newspaper consultant speaking or a jealous woman?" he asked.

"I'm speaking as a newspaperwoman," Jill said.

"I don't think so." Kent closed the car door and rolled down the window. "I think you're letting your emotions interfere with your judgment."

"I'd say that was true in your case, not mine," Jill said angrily.

"Jill, Anita is the kind of woman you'd never want to be, because she isn't tough and take-charge and headed for the top," Kent said. "But she's interested in pleasing a man, and you know sometimes that isn't all bad."

She stood silent as he backed away, then stopped his car. "Aren't you leaving?" Kent asked.

"Sure." She climbed into the Dart and slammed the door, keeping her face averted so he wouldn't see how close she was to tears. As soon as she'd started up her engine, he pulled away.

Jill drove home slowly and sank into the living room couch with a feeling of misery.

Kent's words had hurt more than he knew. He was right about one thing: She'd never want to be like Anita, and she didn't think she could be even if she wanted to. But she'd begun to realize that night they spent together, what it was she'd been hungering for this last year. A man to love, a family of her own, people who loved her and bucked her up when things weren't going well on the job and shared her enthusiasm when they were.

Yes, she wanted to please a man, but she wanted a man who was interested in pleasing her, too, who was as supportive of her life as she was of his. And even though it was like a knife wound to think about it, she had to admit it didn't look as if Kent could possibly be that man.

Chapter Four

Jill arrived at the *Journal-Review* early on Tuesday, looking forward to starting to work with the Sunday editor. However Cindy intercepted her on her way to the newsroom and said Kent wanted to see her as soon as possible.

It was only eight o'clock and the pressure on the news operation wasn't anywhere near its peak yet, but Jill was surprised. She'd gained the impression that Kent considered her role largely window-dressing, and he could hardly be expected to take time from real news to talk to her.

She could see his lean figure through the glass front of his office. He was talking on the phone, leaning precariously back in the swivel chair with his feet on the desk. Despite her determination to remain aloof, she couldn't repress a thrill of response at the sight of his high-boned, handsome face and well-muscled body. Only a few days before, he had swept her into his arms, eased her bikini top down, and traced her breast with his tongue ... but she mustn't think of that.

Jill entered the office and sat down, waiting for him to finish. Kent talked for a moment longer, hung up, and swung his feet down so he sat upright, facing her.

"What do you know about Lloyd Hunter?"

She looked at him, wondering if this had something to do with a news story. "Didn't he used to have a series on television?"

Kent, startled into a smile, shook his head. "You're thinking of Lloyd Bridges and 'Sea Hunt.' No, Lloyd Hunter. He's executive vice-president of CCG."

"I don't know anything about him," Jill said. "What's going on?"

The editor drummed his fingers on the desk blotter. "I'm not sure. But he's coming here today, and I have a feeling the visit isn't purely social."

At least Kent hadn't automatically assumed she had something to do with this, Jill thought in relief. "Thanks for giving me the benefit of the doubt," she said.

"Jill." Kent leaned forward and the intensity in his deep blue eyes sent shivers through her. "Maybe I haven't made myself clear about something. This newspaper means a lot to me, more than anything else in my life right now. It's been my wife, my kids, and most of my friends for the last couple of years." There was a hoarseness to his voice, and Jill knew it came from strong emotion.

"I think I understand that, Kent," she said. "Will you believe, please, that I have no desire whatsoever to hurt you or to see you lose your job?"

He nodded. "Okay, Jill. It's just that Arnold is bringing in the big guns. I can fight for myself out in the open, but I'm no good at backstabbing games."

"You think he's bringing this Lloyd Hunter here because of the Siamese twins story?" she asked, folding her hands in the lap of the crisp white-piped black dress she'd chosen to wear that day.

"That and other things I expect you know about by now," Kent said. "If CCG is this concerned, my job is really on the line."

"I'll let him know my professional opinion, and that's that you're an outstanding editor and that these problems aren't your fault," Jill said.

He grinned ruefully. "I never thought I'd be leaning on you to help me keep my job, but thanks, I appreciate it."

Then he looked behind her and his face lit up. "Here's somebody I'd like you to meet, Jill."

She turned in her chair as he rose and moved forward. Shambling toward them across the newsroom was a little boy about four years old, wearing Winnie-the-Pooh overalls. Following at a more sedate pace was a tall, young woman with bright blue eyes like Kent's.

The editor scooped up the little boy and swung him around, extracting squeals of glee. The woman watched, pleased by the scene, and Jill felt both astonished and left out, like a child with her nose pressed against a window while people within gathered around a sparkling Christmas tree.

She'd never seen Kent with children before, never observed how he beamed in pleasure as he tickled the little boy and the child shouted happily. Finally Kent swung the tot up onto his shoulder and marched back into the office.

"Jill, this is my nephew, Peter," he said, "and my sister Stephanie."

She stood up to shake hands with the tall woman. "I'm very pleased to meet you," she said. "I never knew Kent had a sister and a nephew. I guess editors always seem like they got run off on a printing press."

"This one especially," said Stephanie with a smile. "Listen, Kent, I don't want to take up much of your time. We just happened to be in the neighborhood and I wanted to bring you this." She handed him a small bundle wrapped in white paper.

Kent raised one eyebrow and began to open it. He lifted out a handsome white shirt with intricate colored embroidery across the shoulders. "That's beautiful, Steph. Thanks."

"My husband and I just got back from Mexico," his sister told Jill. "We live up in Palos Verdes, so I don't get down this way very often. Thought I'd risk getting snarled at, which is what usually happens when I disturb my brother at work."

Kent looked sheepish. "Who, me?" he said, handing Peter reluctantly back to his mother. "Thanks, Steph. You three had a good time, I hope?"

"Yes, and there's something else," his sister said. An inner radiance glowed on her face. "We're going to have another one of these little monsters next spring."

A wistful expression Jill had never seen before flickered across Kent's face. "That's terrific," he said, giving his sister a quick hug. "I'm really pleased. Or maybe I should say, it's about time."

"It's about time you were having kids of your own," Stephanie said. "I'll leave you with that parting thought. Now we're off to Newport Beach to see a friend. Jill, nice to meet you."

"I enjoyed it," she said, watching enviously as mother and son sauntered away across the large room. How she wished she were happily married to Kent with one darling child and another on the way.

She glanced up and found him still staring after his sister. "You're really fond of them, aren't you?" she asked softly.

He looked up, his eyes soft and vulnerable. "Yes, I guess I am." He turned back to his desk and shuffled some papers while he returned his concentration to work. "I appreciate any help you can give me with Hunter. You'd probably best head on down to the publisher's office. If Arnold has much time with him alone, he'll probably fill his head with tales of my incompetence."

"Right you are," Jill said crisply and headed toward the front of the building. As she walked past the advertising department, she considered what she'd seen. It was obvious that Kent loved children, something she'd never suspected before. He'd told her in the car that he knew what he was looking for. Was that it?

If only she could be the one, she thought, acknowledging her longing despite the pain it aroused. Even though she knew he was wrong for her, she also knew that Kent was a part of her that she could never get rid of and didn't really want to. If only he could love her the way she was, instead of longing for some clinging, unquestioning woman who would never challenge him or stand on her own two feet.

"He's here," Cindy said as soon as Jill entered the outer office. "Do you think my desk looks all right? I got rid of all the knickknacks like you suggested."

Jill surveyed the office. "It looks sharp, Cindy," she said. "And so do you." The young woman had teamed a button-down shirt with a wrap-around skirt, and while no doubt she'd look better after she'd been able to purchase new clothes, the effect was suitably businesslike.

"Arnold said to show you in right away," Cindy said, hurrying to the door and tapping at it before opening it to usher Jill inside.

The two men stood to greet her. Jill's first impression of the newcomer was that he was friendly and mild-mannered. Lloyd Hunter was in his mid-thirties and of medium height, slightly stocky, with trim brown hair, a well-clipped mustache, and cheerful brown eyes. Despite his conservative three-piece suit, he presented an affable appearance, as if he looked on the positive side of things. That boded well for Kent, she thought.

Arnold made the introductions, and Jill found herself shaking a hand that held hers in a firm grip.

"I'm pleased to meet you," she said as the three of them sat down. "I'd be happy to discuss my preliminary observations with you, if that's why you're here."

Lloyd glanced at Arnold, and the publisher seized the opportunity to speak. "I'm sure he's interested in what you've found so far, but frankly, Jill, Lloyd's here because of the massive foul-ups we've had. CCG is worried."

"They've asked me to form my own impressions," Lloyd explained to Jill. "I'm not here to act as any kind of executioner. It's like our decision to hire you: We just want to be sure everything's in tiptop shape."

"Of course," she said, although she was sure underneath that Arnold had asked CCG to investigate. She found that she was beginning to dislike the publisher. Her first impression had been that he was slick but sincere. Now she was beginning to think he'd jump at any opportunity to make Kent look bad and replace him with an editor who had fewer ethics and was more easily pushed around.

Jill accompanied Arnold and Lloyd on their tour of the building, making additional mental notes of her own about areas for improvement. But her thoughts kept returning to Kent.

Despite his behavior afterward, she found it hard to believe that their night together had meant nothing to him. Neither had ever taken sex casually; he was the first man she'd been with, and he, too, when they'd first become lovers, had held off until their relationship seemed well established.

Thinking about him was like trying to put a jigsaw puzzle together while looking at the pieces from a distance, without being able to move them into place. He'd once cared about her very deeply, she felt certain. It had never made sense to her that he should be antagonized simply because she'd succeeded at her work despite his opposition. Kent was not a petty man, and he'd always been ready to admit when he made a mistake.

She was roused from her thoughts as they approached the features section. Anita, who apparently knew of Lloyd's visit, was working on a page proof with an air of concern that was foreign to her and that Jill gathered was assumed for the executive's benefit.

Lloyd and Anita shook hands, and the woman gazed up at him soulfully in a manner that made Jill want to pinch her. Did she have to curry favor so obviously? If only Kent would see through her and realize that the motives he was always attributing to Jill were in fact more true of Anita.

"If there's anything I can do to help, I'd be more than happy to," the features editor said, leaning against her desk with a seductiveness that Lloyd could hardly have missed.

"Arnold's been showing me around just fine," he said. "Tell me, Miss Ruiz—Anita—how long have you been with the *Journal*?"

"About seven months," she said.

Lloyd picked up a copy of yesterday's section and glanced at it. Jill winced for Anita, although the editor herself didn't seem at all abashed by the fact that a word in a headline had been typoed.

"Anita's one of our newer employees," Arnold interjected. "Kent hired her himself."

Drat him! Jill thought. He was going to make every little error look like it was Kent's fault.

Lloyd was studying the front page of the section. "Someone seems to have slipped up on the proofreading," he said. "There's a typo in a headline, and in the same story a correction has been set in the wrong typeface."

"Oh, I know. Isn't it embarrassing?" said Anita. "I had one of my reporters proof the page yesterday, and I guess that was a mistake. I don't know how she could have missed those things."

Since the writers were all away from their desks, there was no one around to correct her, but Jill felt certain Anita was lying. Surely Lloyd must suspect something, too.

"Tell me, Anita, what do you consider your greatest strength and your greatest weakness as a newspaperwoman?" Lloyd asked.

Jill smiled to herself. At least this man knew what he was doing. He must see through Arnold's scheme.

"My greatest strength? I don't know. I wouldn't want to brag," Anita said. "My greatest weakness is probably that I work too hard. I just won't let up on myself. My reporters all tell me I'm a horrible taskmaster, but that's just my nature."

Lloyd nodded, his face impassive. "Have you ever worked in public relations?" he asked.

"No, I haven't. Why?"

He shrugged. "It seemed to me you would be good at it."

Very diplomatic, Jill thought. It might be true;

Anita would be good at dealing with people, especially men.

They completed their tour, not disturbing Kent and the copydeskers, who were working on deadline now. Arnold had to return to his office for an appointment, so Jill waited with Lloyd in the conference room until the managing editor could take a break.

"I always feel uncomfortable with situations like this, where there's a lot of politics involved," Lloyd admitted when they were alone. "I have to admire someone like Anita, who seems to thrive on it."

Jill nodded, but said nothing.

"You don't like her, do you?" Lloyd asked.

Jill smiled. "Am I that transparent? Really, I'm trying to be objective about her but...she has a lot of weaknesses."

"I suspect you're the most objective person around here," Lloyd said. "I'd appreciate any tips you might have. I'm not talking so much about your professional opinion, which we'll go over later, but things I might be attuned to. CCG plans to keep me down here for a couple of days, and I want to make maximum use of the time."

"I'll do my best," Jill said.

"It might be easier if we talked away from the office," Lloyd said. "I hope you don't think I'm up to anything improper. But I really do think we could talk more freely if we knew no one was going to walk in on us."

"I don't have any problem with that," said Jill, who felt quite comfortable in Lloyd's company. She had recognized immediately that he could never excite her as Kent did, but her bruised ego could use some bucking up. In addition, it would be nice to have someone to talk to who, like her, was on the outside of all the interoffice politics.

"I'll tell you what," she said. "Since you're going to be here for a while, why don't we take in some of the sights together? I haven't had a chance to see much myself. Knott's Berry Farm is just down the road. I thought at first it was some sort of agricultural attraction, but I'm told it's an amusement park with a Western theme. It would give us both a chance to see a little more of Buena Park while we talk."

"That sounds wonderfully educational," said Kent's sarcastic voice from the doorway.

Jill looked up at him angrily. Why did he always have to put her in the worst possible light? No doubt he'd come just in time to hear her suggesting that Lloyd take her to Knott's and had drawn the conclusion that she was playing up to him. Well, let him think so!

"I'm Lloyd Hunter." Lloyd stood and the two men shook hands. "Please don't think Jill was being forward. I feel sort of at loose ends, a bachelor in a strange town for a few days, and she was being helpful."

"Of course," Kent said blandly.

"I'll let you two talk in privacy, if you'd like," Jill said, rising. "I'm sure you've got a lot to discuss."

"Oh, there you are!" Anita popped into the room. "Lloyd, I had a bright idea. Since you're new around here, perhaps you should see some of the sights. I'd be happy to take you around after you get off work today."

"Quick as you are, Jill has beaten you to the punch," Kent said. From the look he gave Anita, Jill gathered that he was fully aware what tricks she was up to. The thing that galled her was that he thought she was on the same plane as Anita.

The features editor looked momentarily uncertain, then plunged in again. "Why don't we all go?" she suggested. "What's on the agenda— Knott's?" Jill nodded. "Oh, I just love going there, and I haven't been in ages! What do you say, Kent, shall we all go?"

The managing editor nodded slowly. "I think I could learn a few things from these ladies. But we wouldn't want to be underfoot, Lloyd."

"Not at all," he said. Jill guessed the executive wanted to take the chance to observe two key staff members when they were off guard.

"Now I really will go and leave the two of you alone," Jill said, looking pointedly at Anita. The dark-haired woman favored Lloyd with one last beaming smile and then followed her out the door.

Mary Jane, whom Jill planned to meet with, had gone to lunch already, so she headed down the street to a restaurant that had a good salad bar. However, after piling up her plate, Jill found herself merely toying with her food and staring blankly out the window.

She wished she could think of some excuse to get out of their outing tonight, but she couldn't think of anything that wasn't overly dramatic or clearly incredible. The last thing she wanted was to spend an evening fencing with Kent and Anita.

Also, even though she was almost certain Kent couldn't be seriously interested in the other woman, she didn't enjoy the prospect of watching Anita bat her eyelashes at him and snuggle against him during the rides.

Jill looked up, startled, as Kent slid into the booth across from her. "Eating alone?" he asked. "I would have thought you'd have wangled yourself an invitation to join Arnold and Lloyd."

"You have some kind of magic touch, you really do," she said, scooping out a piece of avocado. "You always manage to overhear precisely the part that makes me fit your preconceived image."

"I'm trying to be generous," Kent said, mashing together his fruit and cottage cheese with his green salad. "But it's a little hard to see how else one might interpret it. I asked you to speak up for me with Lloyd. Instead, I find you wangling a cozy date." He studied her face and then let his gaze trail down her body insultingly.

Jill was annoyed to feel her nipples tighten beneath his study and wished she could hide the blush that spread across her face as he observed, "You've got a lot to offer, but I didn't expect to find you using it for business purposes."

"That's not fair!" she cried. "You know I wouldn't do anything of the kind!"

"Do I?" His hand slid under the table and ran across her thigh. Jill shuddered involuntarily and, against her will, a responsive heat welled up in her.

She clenched her fists. "Look, Kent, Arnold spent the whole morning trying to make you look bad. When Lloyd noticed a typo in Anita's section, Arnold was quick to point out exactly who hired her."

"Oh?" He studied her thoughtfully, drawing his hand away. "And you thought a little extracurricular cooperation might work in my behalf?"

"Lloyd said he wanted to get my personal impressions of everyone," she answered angrily. "He wanted to talk where we wouldn't be interrupted, and I thought it would be a good chance to speak up for you. I'm sorry I bothered."

"I find it hard to believe you're really as naive as you seem." There was an edge to his voice, but she wasn't sure who it was aimed at. "You're a good-looking woman, and there are a lot of high-powered men who assume bed games are part of their business prerogatives."

"You mean you think Lloyd really was after something?" She couldn't hide her surprise.

"That isn't my impression of him," Kent admitted. "But you're in a vulnerable position. You've staked a lot of your reputation on your work at the *Journal*, and if CCG fires you, it's not going to look good."

"I guess I don't think that way because I've never had anyone in this business expect me to jump into bed with him," she said.

"What happened Saturday was a rare occurrence, then?" he asked.

She wasn't sure whether to be offended. "Yes, on both counts," she said, then explained. "Yes, I don't sleep around, and yes, I especially don't sleep around to get ahead—in case you thought that was what I was doing."

He shook his head quickly. "I didn't think there was anything calculated about it, Jill. It's just that I assumed you—oh, well, what's the difference?"

So it hadn't meant anything special to him after all. He'd thought she was easy prey, and why not? She had to admit she hadn't put up any resistance. Jill toyed with her food some more before speaking again. "Now what are we going to do, Kent? Just go on and forget it ever happened?"

He looked at her with an oddly wistful expression. "I'll never forget it happened, Jill." For a moment they sat staring into each other's eyes, and excitement began to rise in her. She was keenly aware of his strong hand resting on the table and his lean body angled in the booth, separated from hers by only a table. Then he pushed his plate aside abruptly and stood up.

"Kent, what's the matter?" she asked. "Please don't hurry off like that."

He looked at her for a moment, teeth gritted. "Let's just say once lightning has come along and shattered the tree, there's no point in its striking again." He turned sharply and walked away.

Jill sat unhappily, every trace of appetite vanished. Why did he have to keep erecting a wall between them?

For a moment it had sounded as if he was jealous of Lloyd. And what had he meant by his parting remark? She couldn't imagine that he'd been that hurt by the ending of their previous relationship, not when it was he himself who had turned cold and then accepted another job without telling her. Surely he couldn't blame her for their breakup.

Jill left her half-eaten salad and stood up. She would be glad when this job was completed and she could get her emotions back to an even keel. At the same time she knew she would always long for the electricity between them, which she doubted she could ever feel with another man.

After an afternoon of reviewing the policies of the Sunday section, Jill headed back to her apartment to shower and change. She took a while deciding what to wear. She wanted to look her best, especially since Kent would be along, but she had to keep in mind that they'd be doing a lot of walking and riding that might be hard on delicate fabrics.

She selected a pair of plum-colored slacks and a pale lavender blouse with a V neck down to the front buttons, edged by a curling ruffle. It looked feminine and highlighted her curves, although she suspected that next to Anita she'd look pale and overly slim.

To her relief Lloyd arrived alone. He whistled admiringly at the sight of her, then escorted her down to his Porsche convertible.

"I hope you don't mind this change in our plans," he said as he held the car door for her. "I really did want to talk to you alone, but I'm also curious to learn more about Kent and Anita." He swung around the car and slid into the driver's seat. "Are they—I don't mean to pry, but are they going together?"

Jill shook her head. "Not that I know of," she said. "Anita's been making a big deal of flirting with Kent, who seems to put up with it, but I think it's casual at most."

Lloyd nodded as he started the motor and pulled out of the parking space. "Good. Interoffice romances don't always end badly, but they do have a tendency to. The result is usually a lot of tension and the loss of a good staffer."

"That depends on what you consider a good staffer," Jill couldn't resist saying, and he laughed.

"Frankly I suspect Anita's talents could be better utilized in some other kind of job," he said as he drove. "She's got a lot of personality and brass, qualities I can't help admiring because I tend to be on the bland side myself."

"What a thing to say! I always considered that professionals ought to be somewhat reserved."

Lloyd nodded. "That's true. But I'm that way all the time, so I really appreciate people like her. However, she's a lousy proofreader. I checked over some more of her sections this afternoon, and there were a lot of problems."

"Only sloppy editing, lousy proofreading, mediocre layout—I could go on, but it might sound like I'm being catty," said Jill.

"Enough about Anita," Lloyd said. "Tell me about yourself."

They chatted amiably until they arrived at the amusement park, halting across from the full-sized replica of Philadelphia's Independence Hall and walking between rows of homey shops until they reached the entrance to the park itself. There they found Kent and Anita waiting for them.

Kent looked smashing in flared tan slacks and a dark-brown knit shirt with a blue bandanna tied around his throat Western style. Jill longed to be the one standing by his side.

Anita was flashily decked out in a red-checked blouse, unbuttoned to the point of indecency, and a pair of jeans as tight as if they'd been sprayed on. "Looks like the gang's all here!" she said merrily.

They went in together. The next few hours were a test of Jill's self-control, as the features editor alternately clung to Kent seductively and flirted brazenly with Lloyd. Both men seemed to be enjoying the experience, she reflected angrily. Men were such fools for silly women. It hurt that even someone like Kent, whose talent and maturity she admired, should apparently prefer such a blatantly superficial female to her.

She suspected, however, that Anita was maneuvering to attract Lloyd's attention, while not wanting to let go of Kent entirely. The loyalty of an alley cat, she told herself. It did make sense to Anita, no doubt, to play up to the man with the most power. Well, Kent could hardly complain, Jill thought. If he liked a woman who was manipulative and grasping, he could hardly complain when she abandoned him for someone who had more to offer.

Finally Anita contrived to have Lloyd as her partner on the log ride. Jill found herself standing beside Kent in the line.

"We do seem to have an affinity for water, don't

we?" he murmured, slipping his arm around her waist. Jill flushed and looked at the ride in which boats shaped like logs ran through a course inside a "mountain," then plummeted down a "waterfall" into a pool below.

His fingers stroked her side gently, then moved up close to her breast. His grip tightened and she leaned against Kent, weakening before the surge of passion his touch aroused. To her disappointment he drew his hand away, and she realized it was their turn in line.

Anita and Lloyd had gone on ahead with another couple in one of the four-person boats. The family group behind Kent and Jill decided to stick together, and she wasn't at all unhappy that they had one of the boats to themselves.

As their conveyance lurched forward on its track through the water, out of sight of those still waiting in line, Kent turned to Jill. "I have to admit, it's a blow to my ego to see how quickly Lloyd has replaced me in Anita's affections," he said with a wry grin, slipping his arm around her shoulders.

Then he turned and covered her mouth in an eager, demanding kiss that left her breathless. Jill returned the embrace, aware of a suddenly unleashed longing as she reached up to stroke his jaw and trace the line of his ear.

Kent bent over her, his breathing ragged, kissing the vulnerable curve of her throat. His hand cupped her breast, squeezing it gently and probing the responsively erect nipple. Jill moaned.

They were distracted for a moment as the boat raced down an incline. Kent pulled away from her sharply, leaving Jill cold and confused.

"What's the matter?" she asked tensely, yearning for him to encircle her again but afraid of being rejected if she reached out for him.

"I'm sorry. I seem to have gotten carried away. It won't happen again."

He kept his gaze averted, stirring a fiery anger at his unfairly withdrawn affection. "I suppose you think I'm a toy you can pick up and put down whenever you feel like it, don't you, Mr. Managing Editor? Well, I'm not."

"No one would ever mistake you for a toy," he said coldly. "Not Jill Brandon, newspaper consultant. I'm sure you chew men up and spit them out."

"What's the matter, Kent? Can't you stand to see a woman succeed?" she cried, feeling tears swim close to the surface. "Maybe you can't deal with anyone else's success, whether it's a woman or not. Is the *Journal* a handy place to hide away from the world? Are you afraid you can't make it at a larger paper?"

The minute the words were out of her mouth, Jill wished she could call them back. His face turned white and his mouth clamped shut in a thin, angry line.

Their log boat emerged from the watery maze, poised at the top of the artificial waterfall and then plunged uncontrolled into the pool below.

Jill was grateful for the drops that sprayed over them as they hit the water. She didn't want Anita and Lloyd, and most of all Kent, to know that some of the moisture on her cheeks was tears.

Chapter Five

"Suppose we had one person in charge of coordinating both the daily entertainment pages and the Friday Showcase section," Jill suggested, looking up from the stacks of newspaper sections opened on the desk in front of her.

"That presents some logistical problems, but it's a good idea," the Sunday editor said. "We'd have to change the way we're organized, which is okay with me, but Kent would have to approve it."

Jill sighed. "Let's not worry about that right now," she said. "After all, we're just brainstorming. Once I go to him with a complete package, he'll see how it all fits together."

Mary Jane leaned back from her desk and stretched. "My back is killing me," she said. "I'm not sure whether it's this chair or whether I'm getting old. Some days I have to bring a cushion to sit on."

"There's a whirlpool at the apartment complex where I'm staying," Jill said, trying not to think about what had happened there only a few days before. "You'd be more than welcome to come over sometime and use it, if you think it would help."

"I may take you up on that," said Mary Jane.

Lloyd stopped by their desks. After greeting the Sunday editor, he turned to Jill and said, "Could I speak to you for a minute?"

"Sure." Wonderingly, she rose and excused herself, then joined him in the conference room.

"Is anything wrong?" she asked, perching nervously on the edge of a chair.

"Wrong? Oh, no," he said. "I wanted to extend an invitation. Arnold and his wife have asked us to join them Thursday night—that's tomorrow, come to think of it—at a publishers' dinner in Santa Ana. He asked me to invite you myself."

The thought flashed through Jill's mind that Kent would probably read something unflattering into her acceptance, but it seemed impolite to refuse. Besides, she wasn't looking forward to spending the next few evenings alone at her apartment.

There was something else to be considered, too. Kent might belittle her career, but there was no reason for her to do so. As a newspaper consultant, Jill felt it would help to get to know additional publishers. There was nothing wrong with that, except in Kent's eyes, and it seemed as if he would disapprove of almost anything she did.

"I'd love to come," she said, and they made arrangements for him to pick her up the next night.

Yet, Jill reflected as Lloyd departed, he hadn't seemed overwhelmingly enthusiastic about taking her, merely pleasant. She watched him walk slowly across the newsroom and saw him look over at the desk where Anita sat filing her nails over a page proof. Lloyd shook his head, but it seemed to Jill the movement was more indulgent than disapproving.

Even though she knew she didn't really want Lloyd for herself, she couldn't shake off a feeling of disappointment at seeing his interest in Anita. What was it about a woman like that—incompetent, conniving, hostile to other women—that made sophisticated, successful men like Lloyd and Kent interested in her?

Jill forced herself to concentrate on her work for the rest of the day, but it wasn't easy.

Even Cindy's muted but friendly greeting at lunchtime failed to cheer her up, although Jill was glad to note that the young secretary was sticking to her resolve and wearing a businesslike dress.

The daily meeting that afternoon proved a particular ordeal. Anita was glowing in attention from two men, while Kent frowned slightly when Jill walked in and then deliberately ignored her. She thought she detected lines of strain around his mouth and eyes and felt suddenly concerned for him. His entire career was being threatened through no fault of his own, and he couldn't help perceiving her as a member of the enemy camp, she supposed. Then she corrected herself. Yes, he could help it. After all, he should know her well enough by now to respect her integrity.

Jill turned her attention to the others and noted that Cindy was absent. "Isn't Cindy coming?" she asked Arnold.

"No," he answered distractedly. "She had a headache and I sent her home early. She's been working extra hard, and frankly I think she's under some pressure."

"What do you mean?"

He smiled. "Oh, the usual boyfriend problems that young women have," he said. "Nothing serious, I don't think."

Kent began the meeting. The only story of note was one he'd assigned for the Sunday paper. A reporter was preparing an in-depth look at Indo-Chinese gangs that were preying on businesses set up by refugees in Garden Grove and Westminster, south of Buena Park.

"There've been stories before, but no one's been able to get the shopkeepers or the gang members to talk," Kent said. "It's a tight community, and besides, the business people are afraid of retaliation."

"So how did we manage it?" asked Arnold. Jill suspected he wasn't very pleased at seeing Kent manage a scoop.

"Our reporter has an inside source," Kent said. "As a matter of fact, it's her brother-in-law. Her sister married a refugee, and he's helped her win the confidence of people on both sides. Most of them have agreed to talk as long as they stay anonymous, which means it would be hard for anyone else to duplicate our story."

Arnold looked annoyed. "In light of some of the problems that we've had in the past, I certainly hope that's true," he said. "Are you sure we want to hold the story until Sunday?"

"There are still a couple more interviews to go, and then the thing has to be assembled and written," Kent said. "I doubt if we'll have it in hand before late Friday, maybe even Saturday."

The talk went on, but Jill paid scant heed to it. She was too urgently aware of how Kent looked leaning forward in his chair at the head of the conference table, his blue eyes riveted on whoever was speaking. In spite of herself, she experienced a surge of longing, wanting to touch his cheek, to see his sudden, shining smile, and to feel his hand slide down her body. She stopped herself harshly.

At last the meeting was over and the people began to wander out. Kent stayed where he was and Jill remained in her seat also. Finally they were alone. He turned to her with a veiled look and said, "I had something I wanted to ask you."

"Shoot."

"I wondered if you were free tomorrow night," Kent said. "There's a publishers' dinner in Santa Ana that I have to attend, and I thought you might find it interesting."

Relief mixed with disappointment in Jill's veins. If only he'd asked her a few hours earlier!

"I—Kent, I can't," she said.

"Fine." He pushed back his chair and stood up.

"Would you wait a minute?" she snapped. "For heaven's sake, Kent, at least let me give my explanation."

"I'm not stopping you." His arms were folded on his chest, and Jill had the feeling she was being shut out.

"This morning Lloyd came and asked me to go," she said. "He explained that Arnold and his wife had invited the two of us. I didn't have any reason to refuse, so I said yes. If I'd known you were going to ask me, I'd have waited."

Kent sat on the edge of the table, his face impassive. "You didn't owe me an explanation," he said.

"I know I didn't." Jill stared at him pleadingly. "Kent, somehow I always seem to feel as if I'm in the wrong around you, no matter what I do. And I do want to apologize for the crack I made last night. I didn't mean it, about your being afraid of a larger paper. I know you came to the *Journal* because it fits in with your goals, not because you were running from anything."

"That's true," Kent said. "But I have been known to run from things." He met her gaze directly, and she wondered if he was referring to the job he'd taken in Cincinnati, the one he'd left Nashville for. "However I'm not running away anymore. I'm staying here and fighting."

"I hope you win," Jill said. "I'll do whatever I can to help."

He studied her carefully. "Will you? I wish I could believe that."

"Oh, Kent!" She stood up, leaning forward across the table. "Sometimes I could just shake you! Would you please believe I'm your friend ... even if I can't be anything more?" The words were wrenched out of her.

"I've learned not to count on friends," he said. They looked at each other steadily, and Jill felt a shiver run through her at his gaze.

She couldn't help noticing his sturdy, broad shoulders and lean body, and the hot, masculine scent of him so close to her. She longed to be sheltered in his arms, to hear him say that he cared about her and trusted her.

Then she scolded herself angrily. Hadn't she learned by now that there was no protection except in her own independence? Kent had hurt her terribly long ago, and he was hurting her now. She couldn't let herself be vulnerable to him again, and yet she couldn't resist the urge to try to win him back.

"How about if I take a rain check on that invitation?" she said a bit shakily.

His gaze raked down over her body, over the full breasts that grew taut beneath his gaze, the slender waist, and the long, well-shaped legs. "Oh, Jill," Kent groaned. "Why the hell did you have to come back into my life?"

"I certainly didn't plan it," she said. "I didn't even realize you worked here when I took the assignment."

"You must have read about it in the trade journals." He regarded her suspiciously.

She shook her head. "I didn't read them for a long time, so I guess I missed this particular bit of news."

"Why not? Seems to me with your attitude, you'd always be on the lookout for new developments that could be to your benefit."

A trace of contempt laced his words, and her chin came up angrily. "If that's the way you want to think, all right!" she said. "I don't know why I bother trying to explain myself. From now on, you can think anything you want about me. If someone tries to attack me in the parking lot and you walk up while I'm half-undressed, I won't bother to explain! What's the use?"

She stalked out of the room in frustration.

Alone that night in her borrowed apartment,

Jill slept restlessly. Memories of her night with Kent kept seeping through her dreams. They were spraying each other with water in the swimming pool. His legs tangled around hers, and suddenly she was pressed against his well-muscled chest, feeling the silky hair rub against the soft skin of her body. He slipped her bikini top down, revealing twin mounds peaked with passion. Suddenly they were in the Jacuzzi whirlpool, and he bent over her, tracing her nipple with his tongue. She moaned in longing and woke drenched in sweat. It was 3:00 A.M.

Jill finally fell asleep again, but she woke feeling still tired and dragged herself through the next day. Fortunately Mary Jane was easy to work with as they reviewed the Sunday consumer section and explored ways of improving it.

She managed a quick nap after work and then changed into a jade-green evening gown with spaghetti straps and a diaphanous matching cape. Her chestnut hair and amber eyes seemed to sparkle in spite of her depression, and Lloyd looked at her admiringly when she opened the door.

Arnold and his wife were waiting downstairs in their Cadillac. Jill had never met Mary Latimore before and was surprised to find that Arnold's wife was closer to her age than to his. Mary had a mane of tawny hair and dark brown eyes that might have been charming except for the pouting expression on her face.

"Don't you think we could go to some nice restaurant instead?'' she chided her husband in what was clearly an ongoing argument. "The food at these things is so awful, and the people are so boring. Don't you agree, Jill?"

"I suppose it must be very tedious for someone who's not in the business," Jill said cautiously, wondering why on earth Arnold had burdened himself with such an unsympathetic wife.

"It wasn't like this when we were dating," said Mary, leaning over the seat to talk directly to Jill as Arnold steered the car onto the freeway. "We've only been married six months, you know. Then it was, 'Anything you want, Mary.' Now it's all work, work, work."

In the rearview mirror, Jill could see Arnold's mouth clenched tightly. She couldn't entirely condemn Mary, even though she was embarrassing her husband in front of business associates. It appeared that in his eagerness to snare a young bride, Arnold hadn't been above deceiving her about the kind of life he really led. Jill could see how a distinguished older man who drove a Cadillac, radiated power, and cheerfully footed the bill for expensive nights out could attract a butterfly like Mary.

It was a relief when they pulled up in front of the restaurant where the meeting was being held, and Mary quieted down when she saw the elegant decor and realized the food would probably be good, at least.

Lloyd had been quiet during the drive, and Jill saw his gaze sweeping the restaurant as they were led through it into the banquet room. Then he fixed his eyes on one point, and she followed his stare.

Anita, in a fire-engine red, off-the-shoulder dress, stood chatting with a group of men. Next to her stood Kent.

Jill had to bite back her anger. So that was Kent's way of getting revenge. She'd turned him down for Lloyd, so he'd decided to get back at her by taking Anita. Or perhaps that wasn't accurate. He probably hadn't wanted to come alone, that was all. Perhaps he'd only invited Jill for the same reason.

She found her emotions seesawing again and tried to distract herself and Lloyd by commenting on the news of the day. To her relief the ploy worked, and soon they were able to enjoy their conversation.

Since she was not eager for any more of Mary's company, Jill was glad to find that places had been marked and that she and Lloyd were seated at a separate table from the Latimores. Kent and Anita were at a third table, and it struck her that someone must have had the intelligent idea of splitting up co-workers so they could make new acquaintances and avoid boring shoptalk.

Among those sitting near her were the editor of a San Diego daily paper and the publisher of the

Journal's chief rival. Despite her awareness that Kent was watching, she chatted with that gentleman while Lloyd was away from the table for a few minutes. Mostly their talk centered on changes in computer technology that were affecting the editing and design of newspapers.

Both agreed that papers were likely to continue to dwindle in number in the future, to be replaced by written news delivered directly to subscribers' homes via computer. However, the publisher—who was considerably older—thought the change was perhaps a half-century in the future, while Jill believed computers would be as common as television sets within ten to twenty years.

She found the talk exhilarating, which was fortunate, because the after-dinner speeches were deadly dull. A glance showed her that Mary was yawning openly despite her husband's glares. Anita was gazing up at Kent from beneath lowered lashes, whispering intently. She had her hand on his arm and stroked the fabric of his dinner jacket. Jill repressed a primitive urge to walk over and slap her.

The speakers droned on, congratulating various members of the audience whom she didn't know on their various and sundry accomplishments. Jill forced herself to concentrate, linking names to faces for future reference. Like it or not, this was part of her job.

She made some surreptitious notes on a pad

from her purse. Some editors and publishers from Los Angeles and as far away as San Bernardino and Santa Barbara were in attendance, and it made sense to seize the opportunity. It would probably be a good idea to introduce herself around afterward, she thought unhappily. Perhaps she should go back to reporting. Playing politics might suit Anita, but it didn't suit her.

Kent was watching her, she realized as the dinner concluded and informal conversations resumed. Resolutely ignoring him, Jill went about with Lloyd, making new acquaintances.

Mary giggled from too much wine, and Arnold was understandably impatient to leave. Jill agreed readily.

She waited in the lobby while Arnold went to fetch the car. Mary monopolized Lloyd, clinging to his arm and laughing at him flirtatiously. The executive was coolly polite, and Jill wondered if this incident was affecting his judgment of Arnold.

She turned and saw Kent standing to one side. Anita was nowhere in sight, and Jill guessed she'd gone to the ladies' room.

She hesitated, then walked over to him. "I hope you had as rotten a time as I did tonight," she said.

"Yours, at least, appeared to be more profitable." His gaze raked over her coldly.

Jill refused to take the bait. "It is part of my job,

you know, to get acquainted with editors and publishers," she said. "There's nothing in it to be
ashamed of."

"I didn't say there was." His indifference was
maddening.

"Kent, let's not go through this again." She
looked up at him, appealing to his good sense, and
his frown softened. However before he could
speak, Lloyd called out to her that the car was
ready.

"Do you ever get the feeling fate is against
us?" Jill asked ruefully. "Well, see you at the office."

She turned away, then glanced back and was
surprised to see Kent looking at her with a tender
expression. She started to say something until she
saw Anita slide up behind him, linking her arm
through his. Jill let Lloyd lead her out to the car.

She found herself hoping, once she was back at
her apartment, that Kent might call. When the
phone defiantly remained silent, Jill tortured herself wondering whether Kent and Anita were
spending the night together. Then she reproached
herself for underestimating him.

She sat on the couch in her terry bathrobe,
knees tucked up under her, remembering what
he'd been like when they first started dating in
Nashville. He'd never been the suave type like
Arnold, with clothes out of a men's magazine
and, no doubt, a manicured bouquet of roses for

his dates. Daisies and cowboy shirts were more Kent's style when they were having fun together, and she liked him that way. She'd always been acutely conscious of muscles rippling under that shirt and the sparkling spontaneity of his warmly rumpled personality.

Something still flared and crackled between them, and they both knew it. But passion could never be enough—and they both knew that, too, she thought.

On Friday Jill arrived at the office to find Kent already editing busily at the copydesk. She wrapped up her work with Mary Jane and renewed her invitation to use the whirlpool. She'd found the Sunday editor compatible and hoped they could develop a friendship. Jill hadn't made many close girlfriends since coming to California, and she wished she had someone to talk things over with.

She didn't feel up to tackling Anita's department and rationalized that it was a Friday and not a good time to launch into a new project. Instead she observed the copydesk operation for a while, trying not to spend too much of her time staring at Kent.

It was hard not to. He reminded her so much of the way he'd been in Nashville, rapping out orders in one direction, yelling at a reporter or a copy editor on the other side, pounding away at his keyboard. He seemed more alive than usual, his blue eyes flashing, his body tense as if poised for takeoff.

Jill understood the excitement. It was in her blood, too. In the intensity of deadline work, everything else faded away. She'd often been surprised to look up from her typewriter after the pressure was off and discover she was hungry or had a headache.

Something wrenched within her. Damn it, she loved him so much. He was part of her, part of her life and thoughts and desires, and she was part of him. Yet he seemed to nurse some deep-seated resentment of her, a mistrust that eroded any basis for real affection between them. Unless she could figure out what it was and how to breach it within the next week, she would be heading back to Los Angeles very much alone.

Against her will, Jill had to admit she would never again find a man who could move her so deeply. Kent was the standard against which all other men would be judged and found wanting.

She spent most of the rest of the day working in the conference room, drawing together her notes and suggestions so far. The sports department was easy, since it stood largely by itself. There was rarely an overlap with the news pages.

But the Sunday paper and the Friday entertainment section were different. There was overlap not only with the daily entertainment pages but also with Anita's section. Her reporters were often called on to write special features for Sunday, but more than that, Jill knew close coordination between Mary Jane and Anita was going to be necessary.

The Sunday editor had told her she'd tried to work with Anita when the features editor first arrived but had found her uncooperative. Anita didn't like having her best features taken for the Sunday paper.

Jill chewed on the back of her pen. It was hard to deal with petty egos in a newsroom. Prima donnas were out of place. A newspaper had to be a cooperative effort, and readers didn't care about Anita's pride. The fact was that more people read the Sunday paper, so the feature stories had to be extra good.

Lloyd had gone back to Los Angeles for the weekend, and she felt both relieved and anxious. He hadn't consulted her about any conclusions, and she suspected he hadn't wrapped up his report. At the same time she wondered if he were meeting with his superiors about the *Journal.* If Kent lost his job, she knew he'd somehow blame her.

Jill left early, relieved to be away from the suddenly stifling atmosphere at the *Journal* but finding herself at loose ends. It was Friday night, she thought with a trace of bitterness as she shopped for groceries. Here she was with nothing to do but watch television and cut her fingernails.

On impulse she bought a romance novel at the checkstand. If she couldn't live it, at least she could read about it.

The evening passed more pleasantly than expected, and Jill dreamed of happy endings. She awoke feeling more cheerful than she had in some time.

She ate a light breakfast and went for a walk. Might as well pick up the morning papers and see how they'd covered the news. Saturday was a slow day, and since low-ranking editors were frequently stuck with unwelcome Friday night duty, the results tended to be somewhat less than spectacular. She popped coins into two machines and drew out the *Journal* and its rival.

Tucking them under her arm, Jill walked briskly back to her apartment. There she spread them both on the floor and then sucked in her breath in dismay.

Splashed across the top of the rival paper was a feature story about Indo-Chinese gangs.

For a moment Jill couldn't believe her eyes. It wasn't possible that this could have been a coincidence, not after what had happened previously. But she couldn't believe anyone at the *Journal* would have leaked word of the feature scheduled for Sunday.

She read the story, noting that it consisted largely of interviews with police. It was a quickie job, done on Friday. Someone had been alerted.

And even though the *Journal*'s story would be far superior, it would once again look like a case of imitation.

Jill sank back on the couch, trying to sort out her thoughts. What the hell was going on here? She'd never heard of such a thing happening at a newspaper, not consistently. Perhaps someone in the composing room was leaking the news, a typesetter or a proofreader. No, they wouldn't generally see the story until the day before it was run, too late for the competition to match it.

Unless they found the leak and plugged it, Kent was going to be in very serious trouble. It didn't seem fair that his neck should be in the noose when clearly he wasn't responsible, but she knew Arnold wouldn't see it that way. And CCG had to have a scapegoat. They couldn't let things go on the way they were, not with their plans to launch a circulation war.

Mentally Jill reviewed the names of the reporters at the *Journal* and tried to coordinate them with faces. Clearly the reporter who'd written the Indo-Chinese story wouldn't have undercut her own scoop. Someone in the Indo-Chinese community might have called up the other paper, but that wouldn't explain the previous leaks.

She'd never suspected that her consulting job would require that she play detective, but now Jill wished she had all the skills of Sherlock Holmes. She realized the culprit must have a motive—getting a job on a larger paper might be sufficient—and an opportunity, but anyone had that.

He also must have had access to information about the *Journal*'s stories. Technically only those at the daily meetings knew about them, but she couldn't imagine that the editor, publisher, city editor, or the others would slit their own throats.

She jumped at a fierce rapping on the door. Who could that be and why didn't they use the doorbell like normal visitors? Jill peered out with the chain on and was shocked to see Kent standing stiffly in the doorway.

"Kent!" She opened the door. "I saw this morning's paper. I've been trying to figure out who could have leaked it."

"Have you?" He stood there frigidly, making no move to enter the room.

A lump caught in her throat at the implication, but Jill refused to be cowed. "Come in and sit down," she commanded. "All right, Kent, why are you here?"

"Isn't it obvious?" He walked a few paces into the room but remained standing.

"I could guess but I'd rather not," Jill said as coolly as she could. "I don't like to think you've completely lost your mind."

"I was sorry I yelled at you the last time," Kent said. "After I thought about it, I decided it was probably a coincidence that you'd been talking to a certain publisher at the same time a story was being leaked. But this time I don't believe it was a coincidence."

For a minute Jill couldn't imagine what he was talking about. Then she remembered the publishers' dinner and her conversation with the head of the rival paper.

"Honestly, Kent," she snapped. "I can see it won't do any good pointing out that I have a high standard of ethics, so let me appeal to your somewhat questionable intelligence. Do you think I'd be brash enough to leak a story at a table full of newspaper people, including Lloyd?"

"Lloyd was away from the table for a while," he said, his eyes flashing blue fire.

"I suppose I just leaned over and said, 'Remember that hot tip I gave you last time? Well, I've got another one.'" Jill said sarcastically. "Naturally they'd rush to hire an editor who had so little integrity that she'd spy on her own paper."

"It isn't your own paper," Kent said. "You're just hired help for three weeks. Then you're on your way, and we're left to pick up the pieces."

"You had problems before I came here!"

"Only one, and that could have been a coincidence," Kent said. "I've thought about this, Jill. I've tried to be fair. But damn it, the evidence is overwhelming. Who else had an opportunity like that, twice?"

"Anybody who had a telephone!"

He stepped toward her furiously, his hands reaching out and gripping her shoulders so tightly it hurt.

"Let go of me!" She tried to pull away, but he was too strong for her.

"Do you take me for some kind of fool?" he rasped. "I let you do that before, in Nashville, didn't I? You've played on my... my weakness for you to get ahead, and I didn't have the guts to confront you that time. I ran away. Well, I'm not running now. It's your turn to leave."

"What are you talking about?" She tried to ignore the clenched pain in her shoulders as she looked up wildly.

"You're leaving the *Journal*." Kent let go of her roughly and stepped back. "Now. Today. You're going to pack your things, and on Monday you're going to inform CCG that you're dropping the job."

"I'll do no such thing!"

"Oh, yes, you will." His voice was low and determined. "Two can play at this game, Jill. You've leaked my stories. I can spread word of what you've done. Do you think any newspaper in the country will want to employ you when they learn how low you'll stoop?"

She couldn't believe he would actually do such a thing. "But it's not true!" she protested. "All anyone has to do is talk to the publisher of the..."

"Naturally he'd deny it," Kent said. "But if he hires you, that would be a confirmation, wouldn't it?"

"I don't want to work for him," Jill said. "Kent, I'm not going to let you do this to me. I'm innocent. You've never tried to be fair to me, not once. Not in Nashville and not here. You say you didn't confront me. You mean you didn't give me a chance to explain myself!"

"You had every chance," he said. "You just didn't bother to tell the truth."

"You mean the truth as you see it!" Jill felt herself verging on hysteria. He had boxed her into a corner. If she left now, she would be as good as admitting her guilt. If she stayed, he'd spread lies about her. Even if the culprit was later found, a lot of damage would have already been done. And it was always possible they'd never find out where the leak was.

"I've given you your choice," Kent said coldly. She thought she detected a faint gleam of regret in his eyes, but it vanished quickly. "I could simply present this case to your company, to CCG, and to anyone else who's interested, if I really wanted to hurt you, Jill. But I'm giving you a chance to withdraw gracefully."

"You're actually convinced that I did it, aren't you?" she demanded in disbelief. "Convinced enough to go through with this?"

"That's right, Jill," he said. "Maybe you think

I'm trying to get back at you for some personal reason, but it's not true. God knows, I've tried to find reasons to..." He seemed to catch himself and stiffened. "That's beside the point. There's no one else who could be responsible. No one else with a motive or with such an obvious opportunity. You want your fancy job with my competition? Fine. You just go ahead and take it."

"But I don't..."

He ignored her objections. "I'm going to beat you, you and your new employer, fair and square. I won't need to cheat, and I'll make sure you can't. You're going to find out what a really good editor can do."

He turned and walked toward the door, opened it, and then looked back at her. "I'll expect you to be gone by Monday," he said and stalked out.

Jill's anger dissolved slowly into incredulity. Could Kent really be so blinded by his resentment of her that he believed her capable of such a thing? Clearly he did. Yet he could hardly equate her youthful enthusiasm in going over his head in Nashville with deliberate and cold-blooded treachery toward a newspaper she was working for.

Even though she was innocent, he could badly damage her career. How he must hate her! Torn between heartache and dismay, Jill sank onto the couch and closed her eyes, trying unsuccessfully to fight back the tears.

Chapter Six

A half-hour crying jag didn't make Jill feel any better. She took two aspirin against a headache that threatened to blot out her thinking processes.

Leaning back on the couch, she tried to examine the matter rationally, but the only thing she could focus on was that she never wanted to see Kent Lawrence again.

For once she decided to give in to her feelings. This job wasn't worth it. Maybe the whole consulting business wasn't suited to her anyway. She might move back east and look for a newspaper job there.

With a feeling of defeat weighing on her, Jill pulled her suitcase out of the closet and began taking her clothes down from the rack.

The sound of the doorbell set her heart thumping. Could Kent have come back to apologize? Nervously Jill opened the door.

"Hi!" It was Mary Jane Kincaid. "I thought I'd

take you up on your offer to use the whirlpool."
She stopped suddenly. "Jill, what's the matter?
You look as if you've been crying for hours."

"Something like that," Jill admitted, waving
her inside. "I—I've decided to withdraw from this
assignment."

"But why?" Mary Jane sat on the edge of a
chair, studying her intently. "You're doing a su-
perb job, and you're at least halfway done with it."

"Mary Jane ..." Jill couldn't keep her feelings
inside any longer. She had to talk to someone, and
the Sunday editor was the most sympathetic person she'd met since she arrived. "Did you see the
papers this morning?"

"No," Mary Jane said. "What's the matter?"

Jill tossed her the opposition paper and heard
her whistle as she saw the headlined story.

"They did it again, damn them," Mary Jane
said. "But there's no reason for you to feel bad
about it, Jill. No one thinks this reflects on you."

"Kent does."

"Kent?" The editor frowned. Then as she
looked up, she saw the suitcase on the bed
through the doorway. "Jill, you're serious about
leaving. What did Kent say to you?"

"He thinks I did it." Jill felt as if she might
burst into tears again any minute.

"I don't understand."

"He saw me talking to the publisher"—she
nodded at the paper Mary Jane still held in her

hand—"before both of the last leaks. At the Press Club party the first time and at a publishers' dinner the second."

"That's ridiculous." The older woman shook her head firmly. "That's the most absurd thing I ever heard of. Suppose he'd seen me, or Anita, or even Arnold talking to him. Would that prove we were guilty?"

"I guess I'd better explain something." Jill began pacing tensely. "Kent and I worked together before...in Nashville. I was a cub reporter, and when he turned down an investigative piece I wanted to do, I mentioned it to the managing editor. Went over his head, so to speak."

Mary Jane sat listening but didn't interrupt.

"Well..." Jill hesitated, not wanting to get too personal, but finally gave in. "I guess I should mention we were dating at the time."

Mary Jane's expression cleared. "I knew there was some kind of tension between the two of you," she said. "Go on, Jill."

She explained that the assignment had been a success, but he'd never forgiven her for going over his head. "I know I didn't handle it well, but I was just a kid and I felt he was being unfair," Jill said. "But he's resented me ever since, and now he's determined to believe I'm undermining the *Journal*."

"It doesn't make sense," Mary Jane said. "What advantage would there be to you?"

"He thinks I want a job with our opposition," Jill said. "It's not true."

"Of course not." Mary Jane seemed to be mulling things over. "But he didn't hire you, so he can't force you to leave."

"Technically, no," Jill admitted, sitting down on the couch. "But he's threatened to 'expose' me, so to speak, to tell everyone what I supposedly did. I have no way of proving I'm innocent, Mary Jane, and it's possible they'll never really find out who's doing it."

"So you're going to run away." The words were spoken flatly, but Jill sensed an undercurrent of disapproval.

"I—I haven't been able to think too clearly," she said. "I guess I'm really hurt by Kent's attitude. I'm also afraid he could do my career a lot of damage. This kind of reputation can be hard to shake, even if you're later cleared."

Mary Jane tapped her fingers on her knee. "It isn't right," she said. "It isn't good for the paper for you to leave, and it isn't good for you. I'm not sure it's good for Kent either."

"You don't think I did it then?"

Mary Jane looked surprised. "Not for a minute," she said.

"Then what do you think I should do?" Jill smiled ruefully. "Here I am, the big consultant brought in by CCG, and I feel like a kid asking for advice."

The other woman smiled back. "I don't mind playing big sister," she said. "As a matter of fact, I love giving advice. What I think you should do, Jill, is not let that man boss you around as he's trying to do."

"How do I stop him, short of buying myself a gun?"

"You march in there Monday morning and inform him that you're not leaving and he's not circulating any unfounded stories or he'll be sued for slander," Mary Jane said.

Jill chuckled. "I can just see his face. I don't think he'd like that."

"He doesn't have to." Mary Jane's expression sobered. "Seriously, what I think you should do is tell him that you've only got about a week left on your job, and you intend to stick it out. If he has no further leaks after that period, the evidence would point toward you. But I suspect that whoever's doing it isn't trying to point toward you, Jill. This started before you came, whether he wants to admit it or not."

Jill thought over her advice. It would be difficult facing Kent every day, but she could handle that, she thought, repressing the pain she felt at the memory of his angry face. But all she had left was her career, and he might damage that badly.

Mary Jane shook her head. "Let him know that you'll tell Arnold and Lloyd what he's up to. They'll stick up for you, and their word will be taken above his. He could get into trouble, threatening their consultant that way, without anything but the flimsiest circumstantial evidence.''

What Mary Jane said was true, Jill decided, and if she hadn't been letting her emotions rule her head, she would have seen it for herself. Kent had declared open war between them, and she was going to have to shoot back.

''All right,'' she said at last. ''Now why don't we get out there and use that whirlpool?''

Despite her resolve, or perhaps because of it, the rest of the weekend seemed to drag by. Jill picked up two more romance novels and lost herself in them for a while, but she kept wondering why things couldn't work out that way between her and Kent. As it was, he'd gone from being a stranger to an outright enemy.

It had been his choice, she decided. She could see that her behavior in Nashville hadn't been all it might, although she still felt he was responsible for their breakup, but she hadn't done anything wrong here in Buena Park.

She dressed carefully Monday morning in a businesslike white linen suit and fixed her hair neatly. She was going into battle and she at least wanted to look her best.

Jill arrived at the *Journal* at seven thirty, before most of the reporters had wandered in. Kent was already in his office. She strode across the newsroom and saw him look up with an expression of disbelief.

"Good morning." She stepped into his office and closed the door.

"I see you decided not to take my advice." His blue eyes were frosty and a muscle was working in his tanned cheek.

"Advice? I thought it was an edict from on high." She tried to keep her tone impersonal as she sat down uninvited.

Kent didn't answer. He sat regarding her coldly, yet she thought there was a touch of respect in his expression as well.

"I'm not the one who's leaking the stories, Kent, and I'm not going to slink off with my tail between my legs," she said.

"Have you thought about what I said?" He sounded less furious than on Saturday morning, and she guessed that his anger had dimmed somewhat.

"Yes, and I think it was a lot of empty saber rattling," she said, amazed at how steady her voice sounded. "All I have to do is tell Arnold and Lloyd what you plan to do to me, and your neck will be in a sling. Furthermore, they'll both spread the word that I'm not to blame and that you're smearing my reputation falsely, and you'll be the one who gets hurt."

To her surprise, he nodded calmly. "I prefer you like this," he said.

"I beg your pardon?" Somehow she found his smooth indifference harder to take than the passionate accusations of their last encounter.

"You're not playing sweet little girl today," Kent answered. "Now I can see you as you really are—very clever, very tough, and out to get what you want."

Anger rose in Jill with a hot flame. "What is that supposed to mean?"

He glanced past her out the window of the office, and she wondered what the others in the newsroom thought of their early-morning conference. Newspapers were always rife with internal gossip as it was.

"I didn't like dealing with you when you cringed like a hurt puppy," Kent said. "For a while afterward I felt guilty. I even considered apologizing, but then I decided to see what you'd do."

"Thanks. That makes me feel like a guinea pig trying to work its way out of a maze."

"Oh, you've come through better than I expected." Bitterness edged Kent's voice, and his blue eyes were hard. "You've turned the tables on me neatly. You're right. If you go to Lloyd and Arnold, I'll be in trouble. And they can counteract anything I say about you. Your position is foolproof. I'm licked again, and I admit it."

"You're the most infuriating man I've ever met!" Her voice was rising but she didn't care. Let the rest of the newsroom hear her if they wanted! "I couldn't slink away because I'm innocent! But when I decide to stay and fight, you still manage to put me in the wrong! Are you honestly convinced that I leaked the stories?"

Kent's expression softened at the note of pleading. "That's one of the reasons I nearly went back and apologized," he admitted. "I was so angry when I saw the story that I couldn't think straight. It still fits, Jill. You're the only one I know of with the motive and the opportunity. But am I certain? No, I guess not. For your information, I wouldn't have spread those stories about you, although I fully intended to when we met Saturday."

She stared down at her hands for a moment, trying to collect herself. "I suppose I should be happy that I've 'won,'" she said. "But I don't feel as if I've won anything." She looked up tearfully. "Kent, it hurts to think you have so low an opinion of me. I'm an ethical person. I always have been. I've made mistakes, and I haven't always used the best judgment, but I've never done anything intentionally dishonest."

He studied her intently, and for an unguarded moment Jill thought she saw tenderness in his eyes. Then Kent shook his head, as if warning himself of something. "Let's just try to get through the next week the best way we can, shall we?"

"All right." She stood up and forced herself to walk unhurriedly out the door and across the newsroom, although she was shaking inside.

She ducked into the ladies' room and sat on the couch trying to pull herself together. There seemed to be some kind of ambivalence in Kent that didn't make sense. Why hadn't he come back and apologized Saturday if he'd felt like it? It seemed as if he were always testing her, never willing to admit anything positive about her.

The worst of it was, Jill still longed for him, aching in every part of her body for his soothing, inflaming touch. Even as she fenced with him verbally, she yearned for the passion she'd seen in his eyes that night they'd spent together and for a brief moment as they'd ridden through the water at the amusement park.

Yet an impenetrable wall had been erected between them, and she was powerless to bring it down. All she could do was complete her assignment here and then walk out of his life forever.

Jill repaired her makeup and strode back out. Today was the day she had been putting off. She had to tackle the features department.

Anita looked up with a lifted eyebrow as she approached. "Good morning. I suppose it's our turn to benefit from your great accumulated wisdom?"

Jill bit back a retort to the sarcasm. "Why don't we get down to work?" she suggested. "I'm sure we'd both like to get this over with as quickly as possible."

She pulled up a chair and sat down. Anita said nothing. Apparently the other woman wasn't going to lift one finger to help her.

"I'd like to discuss how the department is organized," Jill said. "I'd like to talk about your philosophy of editing and the talents that your staff has available and also about any areas that you think need improving."

"You're the expert on that," said the features editor. Anita was dressed this morning in a vivid blue outfit that hugged her figure and dipped at the neck a bit low for office wear.

"Look, Anita," Jill said. "I can come in here, mark up half a dozen of your sections, and interview your reporters. Then I can make my report to CCG. But I'd prefer to work with you to try to reshape things in a way that you'll be able to live with."

"I don't expect I have much to say about it," said the other woman resentfully. "There's not much point in my cooperating, is there? You're going to write whatever you want to anyway."

It was difficult to deal with someone who had such an unprofessional attitude, but Jill was determined to try. "Frank and Mary Jane didn't feel that way," she said. "Furthermore, I always review my findings and recommendations with the editor before I finalize them. I'm not going to be staying on at the paper, Anita, I'm going to submit my report and leave. You and the others will be responsible for implementing whatever measures are finally decided on, so it's best if you have a lot of input to begin with.''

Anita shrugged. ''Such as what?''

''Such as, are there any weaknesses that you see in the current operation?'' At the other woman's set expression, Jill forced herself to continue patiently. ''For example, perhaps you need more staff. Maybe you'd like to drop a syndicated column or add one. Possibly you need more flexibility with deadlines, or you're having trouble getting proofs back in time from the composing room.'' She was trying to select subjects that wouldn't imply any inadequacy on Anita's part.

The features editor nodded slowly. ''I'd like to do something about the gossip column. It seems pointless to me, and no one here likes doing it, but they've always insisted it's an important part of a local paper.''

Gradually Jill managed to draw more comments, although grudgingly, from Anita, but she found the woman didn't have a good overall sense of what her section should be accomplishing and how to go about it. Kent had certainly erred when he'd hired her, but Jill wouldn't say that in her report. There was no point in antagonizing him needlessly, and she didn't want to give Arnold any more ammunition.

To her relief Anita had to attend a luncheon

meeting and was gone for three hours in the middle of the day, which gave Jill a chance to talk freely with several of the features writers.

She was surprised to find that each of them had some positive things to say about Anita. Apparently the features editor did originate some good story ideas and was particularly helpful in suggesting ways that reporters could get cooperation from difficult sources.

However all of them were dissatisfied with her editing.

"It's not that I don't like her," said a writer named Janet. "But I don't feel that I'm making the progress I should with my work. I'm not getting the kind of criticism I need to improve, and then when I see one of my stories in print full of typos, it makes me feel terrible. Readers always assume the writer's to blame for any errors."

Another reporter, Sam, turned out to have considerable background in film and televison. In fact he wrote most of the material for the Showcase section and entertainment pages. He also expressed an interest in learning more about editing and layout.

When Anita returned from lunch, Jill asked if they could meet in the conference room. The other woman at first protested that she had too much work, but she finally agreed when Jill insisted it wouldn't take long.

"I wanted to consult you about an idea we've

been kicking around," Jill said, trying to make the matter as nonthreatening as possible. "Mary Jane seemed interested, and she thought you might be also."

"Oh?"

"There's been some duplication between the entertainment pages during the week and the Showcase," Jill said. "Also, some local items get overlooked because there isn't one central coordinator."

Since neither was under Anita's direction, she had no reason to feel she was being attacked, but she continued to watch Jill mistrustfully.

"What we've been thinking about is putting both under one editor, kind of a sub-editor," said Jill. "They would operate either under the Sunday editor or you."

"Let me guess," said Anita sarcastically. "It isn't going to be me, right?"

Jill sighed. "The person would still have to be trained and supervised, and since you're so overworked, it seemed to me Mary Jane would be more appropriate."

"I thought so," Anita said savagely. "And whom did you have in mind to fill this position?"

"Sam."

"Of course," the other woman snarled. "You've been looking for a way to gut my department, haven't you? You say I'm overworked, and then you want to take away one of my best writers."

"First of all, most of what Sam writes now isn't used in your section anyway because it's entertainment," Jill countered. "Also, since he'd be relieving the copydesk of handling the daily entertainment pages, they would assume additional copy-editing chores for your section at your discretion. You could hand them inside pages to lay out, for example."

"And lose control over them."

"Not at all. You'd select the material and proof their work." Jill felt as if she were trying to run up a down escalator. "And since Sam would relieve the Sunday section of Showcase, Mary Jane feels they could handle more of their own features, which would let you keep more of your own writers' material."

"You must think I'm really stupid," Anita said. "You're taking a full-time writer away from me and what am I getting in return? A bunch of promises. As soon as it suits their convenience, the copydesk will slack off and I'll be stuck."

"It's only a suggestion, Anita," Jill said as patiently as she could. "Maybe there's a better way to arrange things, but we've got to do something about entertainment. I'd be more than happy for you to come up with a better proposal."

"No, you wouldn't." Anita, who had been puffing on a cigarette, stabbed it out in an ashtray. "You're trying to railroad me, Jill Brandon, and I'm not going to take it."

She stood up and stalked out of the conference room. Jill sat trying to control her own rising anger.

It was insane, having to deal with an editor who behaved like a first-grader. The problem was that Anita was incompetent and had no interest in improving. Well, Jill was going to outline some changes in her report, and right now the idea of moving in Sam to take over entertainment was the best possibility she'd come up with for that particular problem.

Jill reflected with disappointment over her time at the *Journal*. She'd been here since a week ago Friday and had reviewed everything but the news operation itself.

True, Frank and Mary Jane had participated fully, but she'd aroused the enmity of the features editor and the managing editor. Without their support, it didn't matter what she wrote and what CCG or Arnold agreed with. Changes would be sabotaged from within.

Then there was Kent. She couldn't repress the memory of his playfulness in the swimming pool and the yearning for her in his eyes as they'd clung together. But he would never love her, not as she loved him.

Jill rose slowly. It was almost four o'clock and she decided to knock off early. She stepped out of the conference room and looked over to see Kent standing outside his office, surveying the newsroom.

He turned and gave a sharp nod that signaled her toward his office. "I've been looking for you."

Jill bit back an urge to tell him she'd been exactly where she was supposed to be—in her temporary office. "Isn't it time for the daily meeting?" she said.

"Arnold's tied up. Mary Jane had a doctor's appointment, and the city editor went home sick," Kent said. "Under the circumstances, I didn't see much point."

She entered his office and took a seat, determined not to speak until she knew what was on his mind.

Kent closed the door and sat down at his desk facing her. "Anita was just in here," he said.

"Oh, wonderful," said Jill. "Go ahead. Lay it on me."

"You seem to have a talent for antagonizing people, don't you?" he said. "She was very upset. She said you want to take one of her reporters away and that you're trying to undermine her whole department."

"Is that all?" Jill asked. "Nothing about trying to subvert the U.S. government or ruin the ecology?"

Kent chuckled in spite of himself. "I admit it sounded a bit farfetched."

The sudden warmth between them left Jill feeling vulnerable. She longed to lean forward and stroke his face, to have him pull her to him and shelter her in his arms. Instead she forced herself to outline the situation with Anita. "I asked her for alternate suggestions, but instead she flew off the handle," she concluded.

Kent studied her thoughtfully. "Are you sure this has nothing to do with your personal feelings about Anita? After all you aren't proposing to take anything away from Frank or Mary Jane, are you?"

"I'd be more than happy to change my suggestion if I saw something better, but Anita's been completely uncooperative," Jill said.

"I think your attitude might have something to do with that," he said.

Hurt at his championing of Anita, Jill snapped, "I consider her attitude unprofessional, and I question your judgment in continuing to support her."

"I suppose you intend to put that in your report as well?" He rapped out the words contemptuously.

"I was only expressing my personal opinion," Jill said, trying to keep a rein on her temper. "My report will be as factual as possible, and it isn't intended to undermine you. But if you think I'm going to whitewash anything, you're mistaken. You're not perfect, and I'm not going to try to make you look that way."

"So it comes out at last." The glare of his blue

eyes made her shiver. Once again his fury left her feeling rejected and miserable. "All this time you've been expressing your utmost support for me, and you finally admit you don't support me at all."

"That isn't what I said!"

"I seem to forget what you say. It's hard to remember your words when your actions speak so much louder." His sneering words infuriated her, and Jill was trying to think of a retort when she heard a knock at the door.

"Come in!" Kent barked.

Cindy cracked open the door and peeked in. "Is Jill . . . oh, there you are. Could you come down to Mr. Latimore's office? He and Mr. Hunter would like to see you."

"Thank you, Cindy," Jill said, rising. She looked at Kent's grim expression and decided there was no point in arguing further. He'd only twist anything she said.

She followed Cindy to the front office, commenting, "The improvement in you has been remarkable. You've been acting like a real executive secretary."

Cindy smiled wearily. "I'm really trying hard, but it hasn't been easy. Thanks for the praise."

Jill entered Arnold's office, filled with curiosity. She nodded to Lloyd, whom she hadn't seen since Thursday night, and to the publisher. The conversation stayed general while Cindy fetched coffee, and Jill wondered if this meeting had anything to do with the *Journal*'s being scooped again.

As soon as the door had closed behind the secretary, Arnold said, "I guess you both know it happened again. This is hitting us where it hurts most."

Lloyd nodded. "It's become evident that there is some kind of leak, and it needs to be plugged up."

"Any ideas, Jill?"

She shook her head. "I've tried to think who might do such a thing, but so far I've drawn a blank."

"Obviously we need to find out," said Arnold, fingering a cigarette case. "But I don't think the problem is as simple as one unscrupulous individual."

"Oh?" Lloyd watched him noncommittally.

"I think it's a reflection on the whole operation here," Arnold said. "We're gearing up for a very expensive circulation battle, and there's a possibility we'll lose. We need to run a tight ship."

The others waited for him to come to the point. Jill had a sinking feeling she knew what it was.

"Someone's getting access to information they shouldn't have," Arnold went on. "We don't know what else has been leaked—circulation information, editing procedures, even our plans for the future."

Lloyd spoke up. "Are you suggesting some

type of security system? I don't see how it could catch someone who might be revealing their information over the phone or in person. It's not as if any documents had been stolen.''

Arnold shook his head. "There's one person who's responsible for what goes on inside a newsroom, and that's the managing editor. Unfortunately although I don't question Kent Lawrence's ability, I do question his loyalty.''

"On what grounds?" Jill demanded. "You certainly can't believe he's leaking those stories himself.''

"Not exactly," Arnold said. "But it's no secret that he resents me and, I suspect, CCG itself. His allegiance was to the former owner, and he's particularly unhappy with having this paper in the hands of a large corporation. I think he'd like to see it sold to another individual who would let him run things his own way.''

"I can't believe that," said Jill. "Hardly any newspapers are individually owned these days. He'd be foolish to expect that to happen, even if CCG did sell.''

"Let me get this straight," said Lloyd quietly. "Are you suggesting that the managing editor is somehow responsible for these leaks?''

"Indirectly at least," Arnold said. "If he's not behind them, he's allowing them. He's not running things tightly. He's letting information get out into the newsroom and perhaps the back

shop. From there, who knows? I believe Kent
wants CCG to give up the idea of a circulation
battle because he knows we wouldn't bother to
hold on to a small paper like this with no hope of a
major expansion.''

"Are you making a recommendation?" Lloyd
asked.

Arnold swallowed and nodded. "I'm sorry to
do this, but I think CCG should consider termi-
nating its relationship with Kent Lawrence."

"That's a euphemism for firing, isn't it?" said
Jill. Her instinct was to leap to Kent's defense, but
she must keep her approach businesslike. "I disagree with your conclusion."

"Tell me why, Jill," said Lloyd, turning side-
ways in his chair to face her.

She marshaled her arguments carefully. "I've
worked with Kent before, and I've always observed him to have the highest integrity. And I
know he's been very upset by these leaks. He
feels they reflect badly on him, and that's not
something he takes lightly."

Lloyd nodded slowly. "Anything else?"

Jill tried not to think of the irony of the fact that
Kent had tried to make her give up her job and
now she was helping him keep his. "I think we
should make every effort to find out who's really
responsible before we jump to any conclusions."

"I agree," Lloyd said, to her immense relief. "I

understand your thinking, Arnold, but I think you're letting your attitude be colored by your personal antagonism. Firing a man is a serious business, and it's not something we should do without proof.''

From Arnold's expression Jill knew he was sorely disappointed, but he saw the futility of further argument. ''Very well. I won't push the matter at present,'' he said. ''But, Lloyd, I hope you'll keep this in mind if we continue to have problems. It may be that Kent isn't intentionally undercutting us, but I think he wants CCG to give up the paper, and he's at least willing to turn a blind eye to some misconduct.''

''We'll see,'' Lloyd said. ''Jill, you'll be here the rest of the week? Good. Keep your wits about you. You've got the best chance of any of us of sniffing this thing out.''

''I'll do everything I can,'' she promised.

''One more thing,'' Lloyd said. ''I'm sure I don't need to mention that nothing is to be mentioned to anyone about what has been said here this afternoon.''

Jill and Arnold nodded.

''I'll be back up in LA, but I'll keep in touch,'' Lloyd told them. ''Be sure to give me a call if anything breaks.''

''Of course,'' Arnold said.

Jill headed out of the office feeling depressed.

She'd just helped save Kent's job, but there wasn't a thing she could do to let him know. He'd go on believing she was his enemy, and there was no way to disprove it.

Chapter Seven

Kent was still working in his office when Jill walked by to collect her briefcase from the conference room. He glanced up, then jerked his chin to indicate he wanted to see her.

Not again, she thought, gathering her things and then making her way into his office. She felt drained after her earlier fight with him and her confrontation with Arnold. If Kent wanted to resume their quarrel, she was afraid she might burst into tears.

"Mind telling me what's going on?" he said as she slid wearily into a chair. His tone was rough-edged, but the expression in his blue eyes was worried.

"I'd like to tell you all of it, but it's supposed to be confidential," she said, and then bit her lip. She'd already revealed more than she intended.

"That must mean it was about me," Kent said.

"Come on, Jill, don't you think I have a right to know?"

She straightened, invigorated by anger at being once again put in a no-win position. If she told him what had been said, she'd be violating a confidence. But if she didn't tell him, Kent's tone seemed to imply that she was deliberately keeping him in ignorance.

"Basically they're worried about the leaks," she said, avoiding a direct answer to his question. "They can't figure out who's responsible, and they think it's important that we plug the leak."

"It took Arnold and Lloyd and you, all three, to figure that out?" he replied sarcastically. "Amazing."

"Stop it, Kent!" she cried. "You've been baiting me all day and I'm fed up!" She rose to leave but, in her haste, dropped her briefcase. It fell open, scattering papers all over the floor. "What a mess!"

"Jill...I'm sorry." His tone was rueful, and when she summoned the nerve to look up and meet his gaze, she found his eyes meltingly sympathetic. "Here, I'll get it. And you're right. I've been taking things out on you. If it's any consolation, I've been chewing out everyone else in the newsroom, too."

He knelt to pick up the papers, and Jill slipped down beside him. "I don't know why I'm feeling so emotional," she found herself chattering as she stuffed a marked copy of the features section back into the briefcase. "I don't usually act this way on assignments. This has been a disaster from beginning to end."

"What do you mean?"

"Oh, everything's gone wrong!" she cried. "I've antagonized you, and Anita, and here I am acting like a clunky overgrown schoolgirl. Somehow when I'm around you, I still feel like a kid reporter. You must think I'm really a goofball."

"Not at all." His voice softened as he reached out for more papers.

His hand brushed hers, and Jill found herself longing to press against him, to be pulled against his broad chest and held until she forgot where she was and what she was there for.

She looked up and met his gaze. Kent's eyes half closed and he leaned forward, covering her mouth with his, his hands reaching up to grasp her shoulders. Jill moaned as his tongue tasted the corners of her mouth and one hand stroked down her back, raising quivers of desire.

He drew his face away slowly, then leaned forward again, his lips whispering against her hair. "Why do we torture each other, Jill? What is it that keeps drawing us together? God, I wish you'd never come back into my life. Or maybe I wish you'd never gone away."

"I didn't go away," she murmured. "Oh, Kent, why did you leave like that? When I found out you'd taken that job in Cincinnati and hadn't even told me, I thought I would die."

She bit off her words as she saw him fight back the tenderness from his expression, replacing it with a cool distance. "There's no point in bringing up dead issues, is there?" he said tightly. "We both know that leads nowhere."

What an idiot she'd been to reveal her feelings! "I guess we both got a little carried away," she managed to say, pushing the last of the papers back into place and standing up. For the first time she remembered that they might have been seen, but a glance over one shoulder reassured her that there was no one close enough to have spotted their encounter on the floor. Of the few people left in the newsroom, no one was paying them the least attention.

"It must be the strain around this place," Kent continued. "It's beginning to affect everyone. Sometimes I say things that—well, I don't know where they come from."

Jill could only nod helplessly, agonizingly aware that only moments before his tongue had been sending flames through her body. "Kent, I'm not trying to hold back information from you. I don't think anything was said today that would surprise you. And I meant what I said before, that I'll do what I can to help you. For some reason you seem to have trouble trusting me, but I'm honestly doing my best to help."

"Am I interrupting anything?" Jill turned at

Anita's cutting tone and realized the other woman had cracked open the door. Thank heavens she hadn't come a few minutes earlier!

"I was just leaving," she said.

"So glad to hear it," replied Anita. Jill forced herself to walk out of the office without looking back to see Kent's reaction.

She wasn't kept in suspense about the purpose of Anita's visit, for the features editor's voice carried clearly through the closed door before Jill had taken more than a few steps.

"Well? Did you set her straight about her pushy little plans for getting my department?" The tone was shrilly demanding. "It sounded like things were awfully cozy between you two when I came in."

Jill hurried away, her heart contracting at the thought of overhearing Kent's response. She didn't want to listen to him side with Anita and relate how he'd accused Jill of being unfair. How could he stand that woman? Well, only a few more days and she'd never have to see either of them again, she reminded herself.

Scarcely noticing where she was going, Jill walked past the advertising department and into the front lobby. She was so preoccupied that she didn't notice until the last minute that Cindy was racing out of Arnold's office and across the lobby toward the ladies' room on a path that brought her smashing into Jill.

Both women were knocked breathless to the

floor, scattering purses and briefcase about. Fortunately this time the papers stayed largely in place.

"Oh, I'm sorry!" wailed Cindy. "Are you hurt?"

"Just my proverbial dignity, and there wasn't much left of that to begin with," Jill said, wincing slightly as she stood up. There was a run in her stocking, and she could feel a bruise blackening and bluing on her thigh, but there was no point in dwelling on it.

"Everybody all right?" called the switchboard operator from the other side of the lobby.

"Sure. Just fine," muttered Cindy. A lost look in her eyes, somewhere between hurt and anger, told Jill she was very far from being just fine.

"Something you want to talk about?" she asked gently. In her own distraught condition she wasn't sure she could be of much help, but it went against the grain to walk away and leave Cindy so unhappy without trying to help.

"Yes, I guess I would," the younger woman replied, and they walked together into the rest room, settling down side by side on the couch.

"It's Tim," Cindy said, pulling a tissue from her purse and poking at something in the corner of her eye.

"Your boyfriend?"

Cindy nodded. "It sounds so silly. We had a fight. Jill, I don't understand him. I'm only trying to do my job well. You'd think he'd want me to succeed, wouldn't you?"

"That would be the natural assumption," said Jill. "But men don't always think the way we do. Maybe he's afraid you're putting your job ahead of him?"

"I guess that must be it." The blond girl took out a compact and began repairing the damage to her makeup. "He can't understand why I won't yak on the phone like I used to while I'm at work."

"Can't you talk in the evening?" Jill found herself wishing that the problems between her and Kent were that simple.

"No, he's working nights right now, so it is kind of difficult," Cindy said. "We only see each other on weekends. I've tried talking to him during my lunch hour, but a lot of times that isn't convenient for either of us. You'd think we could get through a few days without talking, but he gets so upset. I probably should feel flattered, but to tell you the truth, it's making me feel kind of trapped."

"Have you told him that?"

Cindy sighed. "Yes. Boy, did that make him mad. I don't know what I'm going to do. And it's only Monday, so we won't really be able to get things squared away until next weekend. Anyway, I don't mean to get your shoulder soggy weeping all over it. I'm okay now, Jill. Thanks for listening."

"I don't feel like I did much, but you're more than welcome." Jill smiled at her and was relieved to see Cindy grin back.

She walked back into the lobby and watched Cindy disappear into Arnold's office. It was almost five thirty, Jill saw on the wall clock, but she was distracted again from leaving as she noticed a copy of the day's paper on the front counter and realized she hadn't reviewed it yet.

A quick glance should be sufficient. Jill flipped through, noting a particularly good layout on page three. She turned to Anita's section, but before she could do more than glance at it, she became aware of high-heeled footsteps clicking toward her.

It was the features editor herself. "Could I talk to you alone, please?" Anita asked in a strained voice.

"Sure," Jill said, repressing a weary sigh. "I'll tell you what. I've been trying to get out of this building for an hour without much luck. How about if we go somewhere else—Sparky's, maybe?"

"Fine," the other woman said. They walked out together into the late afternoon sunlight. Jill couldn't think of anything to say as they crossed the parking lot, and she decided there was no reason to make small talk anyway. Whatever was on Anita's mind, it certainly wasn't pleasant chitchat.

They slid into a booth and placed their orders,

Anita deciding on rosé wine and Jill choosing white wine. She nibbled uncomfortably at the corn chips on the table, waiting for the features editor to begin.

"I guess you win," Anita said at last, bitterness darkening her words.

Jill finished munching a chip before responding. "I give up," she said. "What did I win?"

"Oh, don't try to play cute," snapped the other woman. "We both know what's going on here. You're trying to undermine my work, and you've succeeded."

Jill was grateful for the interruption as the waitress served their drinks. Anita always managed to rub her the wrong way, but while it might give her a certain instant gratification to snarl back at her, Jill knew she'd regret it in the end.

"Look, Anita, you've misunderstood what I'm doing here," she said. "My job is to suggest ways of changing the *Journal-Review* that hopefully will improve it. While I don't pretend to be above human foibles, I try very hard not to let my personal likes and dislikes enter into my recommendations."

"You and Kent must have been reading the same book," Anita said. "*How to Give Uplifting Speeches to Your Inferiors* or something like that."

"I'm going to assume that you asked to talk to me for a reason," Jill said frostily. "I'm going to further assume that that reason wasn't just to snipe at me. So why don't you tell me what this is all about, and then we can take it from there."

Anita nodded. "My family always said I was hot-tempered. All right. When I talked to Kent earlier today, he agreed with me that it wasn't fair to take away one of my staff members. He said he would talk to you about it."

Jill nodded. "And he did. So then what happened?"

"When I went back to find out the upshot, he . . ." Anita paused and took a drink of her wine. "He told me you were doing your job the best way you could and that I was being paranoid. Paranoid! How dare he use a word like that to me?"

"Kent actually backed my idea?" Jill shook her head. "I'm surprised. Frankly, I thought he disagreed with everything I ever wrote or thought in my entire life."

"Men. Who can understand them?" Anita stared into her wineglass. "He's never given me any trouble before. Why should he take your side against me? What's going on between you two?"

"Mostly a lot of arguing and fighting," Jill said. She waited, suspicious of the moderation in Anita's tone. The other woman seemed more reflective now, but Jill expected her to lash out again at any moment.

To Jill's surprise, Anita remained calm. "What do you think about Lloyd?"

"Lloyd?" Jill said. "Well, he seems nice enough. A bit on the bland side."

"Did he say anything about me?"

Jill searched her memory. "He thought you were good at dealing with people. In fact I believe he said you'd do well at public relations."

"Yes?" Anita was clearly searching for something more.

"He said he admires people like you, who are"—she selected the word carefully—"outgoing, because he's so reticent."

Anita nodded. "That's good."

"Mind telling me what this is all about?"

"Nothing, yet." Anita finished her wine in a gulp and added without looking up, "You know what they say. If you can't lick 'em, join 'em."

With that ambiguous remark, she placed some money on the table and departed, leaving Jill to finish her wine in puzzled solitude.

The evening was slightly chilly, a sign that even in Southern California, winter—or what passed for it here—was not far away. Nevertheless Jill decided to take a dip in the Jacuzzi whirlpool bath, wrapping a large towel around her on the way out and hopping gratefully into the steaming water.

She let the swirling jets cut off the rest of the world. As her body relaxed, Jill noticed she was wearing the same bikini she'd chosen that night with Kent.

The realization made her shiver despite the penetrating heat of the whirlpool. She had an instant tactile memory of being held against him in this very spot, his skin yearningly close to hers, his lips demanding a response as he slid the bikini strap from her shoulder and bent down to claim her nipple with his mouth.

Instinctively she moaned, missing him so badly it hurt. It wasn't fair that she should need him so much, when she could never have him. Her intellect told her that night together had been a mistake, but something inside her refused to believe it. Even if she had nothing more, she knew she would cherish that memory forever.

After a while a middle-aged couple joined her in the pool, the woman wearing a lumpy blue one-piece suit and a yellow bathing cap with colored plastic flowers on the front. Jill decided it was time to return to the apartment and get some sleep. She had a feeling she was going to need it.

However the next day wasn't as difficult as she'd expected. Jill began by observing the copydesk in action and found the editors accepted her readily into their good-natured joking. She felt pleased that she was able to discern several easy changes that would streamline the operation and save wasted energy. Kent couldn't help being impressed by that fact when he finally read her recommendations, she told herself, not if he was being truly objective.

Kent himself joined the copydesk just after ten o'clock, in time to supervise the layout of the street edition, and she was able to focus on him in action.

He radiated an unselfconscious masculinity in the decisive movements with which he outlined the placement of type, photographs, and headlines on a lined page, demanding information from the other editors without looking up. From time to time he paused and cracked a joke, which was met by an appreciative chuckle from his colleagues.

He had changed from the days in Nashville, Jill decided, experiencing a pang that she hadn't been there to watch him develop. He seemed more confident and less harsh, and a glance over his shoulder revealed what she'd suspected before: The unusually good layouts she found in the paper from time to time were Kent's.

Jill was also impressed by the way he dealt with a reporter whose story had holes in it. Kent was able to tell the young man in a few words exactly what was wrong with the article and how to correct it, without making sarcastic remarks as he might have done in the past.

As the first set of page proofs came in through a pneumatic tube and were distributed to the copy editors for checking, Jill allowed herself a moment to react to Kent physically.

As he slashed down the page with a blue pencil,

the intensity of his concentration chiseled inviting hollows in his high-cheekboned face. She longed to trace them with her lips, to feel him turn toward her and seek her mouth with his, to explore the contours of her body with skilled hands...

I've got to stop this! Jill scolded herself. *What if he looked up and realized what I was thinking?* She blushed at the thought.

For the rest of the morning, she tried to distract herself by asking questions and moving about the copydesk area to observe what everyone was doing. Once the reporters were off deadline, she chatted with several of them about ways they thought the paper could improve its coverage and story quality.

Kent had hardly seemed to notice her presence at all, so she was taken by surprise when he looked over at about one o'clock and called, "Hey, Jill, you want to get some lunch?"

"Sure," she responded lightly. "Shall I bring my notes?"

He shook his head and pushed away from the desk. Jill glanced at Anita, who had been uncharacteristically subdued all morning, but the features editor was talking on the telephone and appeared not to have heard.

They took Kent's car, and he selected a restaurant Jill hadn't seen before, several blocks away. It was a steak and seafood place with lots of wood paneling and upholstered booths, as well as a moderately priced lunch menu.

"I have no idea what mahi-mahi is but the name is intriguing," said Jill once they were seated. "It sounds like either a pagan ritual or something that wears a hula skirt and shakes its hips."

"Actually it's fish," Kent said, studying his menu. Jill tried to read his expression but couldn't.

She decided on the mahi-mahi, and he selected a steak sandwich, ordering wine for them both as well. Jill leaned back in the booth, determined to let him set the tone of this meeting, since he'd asked for it.

"Would it be premature for me to ask what your observations are from this morning?" said Kent when the wine had been placed before them.

Jill debated a moment, staring out the window into a courtyard-style garden filled with ferns and an enchanting bird of paradise bush, its long-stemmed orange and blue flowers looking amazingly like the heads of brilliantly plumed birds.

"I hadn't really drawn any conclusions yet," she said. "There are a few suggestions I'll want to make, of course, but I haven't found any major criticisms. Your news operation is the strongest part of the paper."

"Then what *is* wrong with the *Journal-Review*?" he asked gravely, looking directly into her eyes.

"You've made it plain from the beginning you thought there was a lot wrong with the paper, and Arnold certainly agrees with you," said Kent. "The leaks aside, what do you think it would take to make this paper into one that neither he nor you could find fault with?"

"Boy, that's a tall order," said Jill. "You're asking me for my entire report."

"That's right," Kent said. "I don't want it to catch me off guard. Let's just say I'd like to get the jump on Arnold on this one."

She hesitated. "You're not just asking me this to pick a fight? I'm not trying to be difficult, Kent, but sometimes it feels as if you only want to hear my ideas so you can tell me what's wrong with them."

Unexpectedly he chuckled. "My intentions are entirely honorable. Here, I'll prove it to you."

Before she realized what he was up to, he had slid out of his side of the booth and moved in next to her, deftly rearranging the place setting as well. "How's that?" he asked, looping one arm around her waist.

Jill had a hard time speaking through the sudden pounding of her pulse. "Not—not exactly businesslike, is it?" she stammered.

"Absolutely," Kent said, amusement glinting in his blue eyes. "I'm trying to pry information out of you, and this is the most efficient way I can think of to do it."

"Using your charms as a weapon, eh?" she managed to tease. "Sort of a 'Mata Harry,' if you take my meaning."

Kent chuckled. "Now if I were really unscrupulous, I might do this." His hand, hidden by her body from the other diners, caressed the curve of her waist, the thumb teasing upwards to the swell of her breast.

Jill's eyes closed instinctively. Part of her wanted to fight him, to preserve what dignity she had left, but her yearning body betrayed her. His touch was like fire, melting her resistance as he caught the tip of her breast between his thumb and forefinger and squeezed gently.

"Kent," she whispered. "You shouldn't be ... it's not right ..."

"I'm doing the best I can." His voice was husky. "Let me put it this way." His other hand reached under the table and stroked her leg, reaching up beneath the skirt to the yielding softness of her thigh.

"We ... not here." It was an effort for her to speak and to remember that they weren't in private.

"Hmm." He hesitated and then slowly pulled his hands away. Jill, aching with a sudden sense of aloneness, leaned against him, rubbing her cheek against his shoulder. Kent leaned over and kissed the tip of her nose.

"Let's see now, who had the mahi-mahi?" The

waitress, with professional dispatch, set the dishes before them, and Jill drew away reluctantly.

The next few minutes were occupied with the business of eating. The fish was delicious, but after the first few bites Jill found it hard to concentrate on what she was tasting.

"I wouldn't want you to think I behave like this normally," Kent said after a few minutes. "Generally I'm the best-behaved fellow you'd ever want to meet."

"I'm not sure I'd want to meet you if you were well behaved," Jill shot back, and he laughed.

"Well, that's comforting. So I haven't irreparably offended you?"

"You know you haven't." Jill poked at a sprig of broccoli. "But I have to say all this emotional seesawing has been hard on my psyche. One minute you're every woman's dream, and the next you turn into King Kong on the rampage."

"I thought that *was* every woman's dream," Kent responded with a grin.

Jill kept busy for a few minutes dissecting her fish, then decided to be frank with him. "I'm having a hard time knowing how to deal with you," she said. "One minute you act like you hate me and the next . . . well, the next minute you're my lover."

Kent's expression sobered. "I haven't been very consistent, have I? I seem to be having a hard time controlling myself around you."

"I'm not necessarily complaining," she said.

"I know. But I'm having some trouble puzzling you out, too," he said thoughtfully. "Sometimes when you get on your high horse, you remind me of things... well, there's no point going into that. Let's just say it doesn't bring out the best in me. But when you're not so uptight about being Miss Superior Professional, I must confess I find you downright hard to resist."

His comments were anything but reassuring, Jill thought with a sinking feeling as she sipped her wine. If she interpreted them correctly, what he was really saying was that he didn't like her as an adult, independent woman, but he still liked the part of her that was soft and clinging, the way she'd been when they first met.

A yearning swept through her. Why couldn't she be like that all the time? Would it be so terrible to be taken care of and loved? Maybe Kent would fall in love with her if she gave up her career or settled for a job that didn't require her to be assertive.

But even as she momentarily contemplated giving in, she knew it was a lost cause. She could never be that way, not for very long. After a while her own forthright, adult nature would push forward, and the result would be frustration, anger, and the end of their relationship.

He'd accuse her of having tricked him, and he'd be right. She'd accuse him of not loving her for herself, and she'd be right. And the whole affair would be wrong, wrong, wrong.

"I think we'd better get back to business," Jill said.

"Okay." Kent was paying a lot of attention to his sandwich, and she wished she knew what was going through his mind. "Think you could give me a quick run-through of the highlights of your report?"

"There are a lot of little specifics, but you could find things like that wrong at any newspaper," Jill said. "But I have to admit I do think there's a basic problem."

"Go ahead," Kent said. He was listening intently, but to Jill's relief at least he didn't look angry.

"The paper needs more of an overview," she said, wondering how long it would be before she managed to offend him. "You're very strong on the news operation. The problem is most people today get their headline news from radio and television."

Kent nodded. "We all know about that."

"So while news is important, especially local news, people tend to read a newspaper for a lot of other reasons," Jill continued. "Advertisements, features, advice columns, news about specialized subjects such as real estate and local business, accounts of events coming up in their area, as well as in-depth background on the news that they can't get on television."

Kent was watching her expectantly, so she took a deep breath and went on. "A newspaper has to have an overall sense of what part each of these elements plays. That means—well, to put it bluntly, the features section isn't window-dressing. It's part of a larger package, and it all needs to be integrated."

For once she seemed to be getting through to him, and Jill continued talking as they finished their meal and moved on to coffee. Kent asked questions from time to time and continued to respond reflectively as she outlined ways in which the newspaper could be reshaped and rethought to present a better-rounded whole.

"It doesn't have to be the journalistic version of *People* magazine, as a certain editor commented when I first came here," she concluded.

"I think I'm beginning to understand what you mean." Kent shook his head. "You know what's really painful about all this? I think you're right. And I've been too bullheaded to see it. Well, it's after two o'clock. I guess we'd better be getting back to the paper before they send out an all points bulletin for missing persons."

It was with very mixed feelings that Jill returned to her seat in Kent's car and watched his firm grip on the steering wheel as he maneuvered out of the parking lot.

She'd won. Hard as it was to believe, Kent had accepted her point of view and even acknowledged that he'd been in the wrong.

That should have made her feel wonderful. But since they'd started talking seriously, he hadn't once tried to touch her or joke with her.

Deep down inside, Jill had to admit she didn't feel as if she'd won at all.

Chapter Eight

The rest of the afternoon passed smoothly. Kent listened carefully to all of Jill's comments, readily answering her queries and responding with further questions of his own.

They reviewed the methods of assigning reporters to beats, what each reporter was responsible for, and how each was performing. It was the type of business relationship Jill was used to having with editors, but somehow this time she wished it weren't quite so businesslike.

Kent hardly seemed aware of her as a woman, but she couldn't suppress a physical response whenever he came close. It was unfair that men should be able to divorce themselves from their feelings so easily!

Surprisingly Anita didn't interfere at all. She left the office early for an interview without a single snide remark to Jill.

By the time Jill and Kent had reached the point

of exhaustion, it was six o'clock and almost everyone else had gone, except for a sportswriter preparing to cover a game that evening.

"I'm starved," Kent said. "That steak sandwich was pretty substantial, but there's a limit to everything."

Jill nodded, wishing she didn't have to face going home to an empty apartment. She didn't feel like cooking, but she didn't feel like watching television and eating a frozen dinner either.

As if reading her mind, Kent said, "Why don't we go someplace nice for a change?"

"What, lunch and dinner both in one day?" Jill managed to joke. "I suppose that's an appropriate symbol of our new accord. Aren't there tribes where breaking bread together makes you brothers for life?"

"Ah, yes, the cult of the cholesterol kin," quipped Kent. "Let's get the logistics of this worked out. You go home and change. I go home and change. I harness my llama and pick you up. How does that sound?"

Jill agreed willingly. But a short time later, trying to decide between a crisp suit and a softer, silkier dress, she sank down onto her bed miserably.

Spending time with him now could only prolong the agony. Perhaps this evening she'd be the woman he wanted again, but then at the office tomorrow it would all be different.

She debated briefly phoning him and calling it

off, but she remembered with an unexpected feeling of relief that she didn't have his phone number.

Anyway, at the rate they were progressing, she'd probably be able to wrap up her hands-on work at the *Journal* tomorrow. All that would be left would be to organize her notes, draft her report, run it by the editors involved for comment, and then finalize it. There was no reason she couldn't leave Buena Park by the end of the week. So she might as well sit back and enjoy tonight while she was still around.

Jill opted for the soft, flowing dress made of a loose rust-colored fabric and shaped to emphasize the contours of her body without hugging them indecently. She studied herself in the mirror, noting with dismay that her eyes were shining at the prospect of one more evening with Kent.

Honestly, she scolded herself, he was just hungry and he probably doesn't like to eat alone. You're the salad dressing, not the dessert.

She found herself listening closely, starting up whenever she heard a car door slam outside, until at last masculine footsteps ascended the stairs and there was a rap at the door.

Jill forced herself to walk slowly across the living room and open the door casually.

In the fading daylight the glow from the room glinted on Kent's slightly crooked smile as he looked at her. "Mmm. Very nice," he said.

"Oh, this is just a disguise," Jill responded. "I

try to fool people into thinking I'm a woman instead of an executive.'' She wished her breath didn't come so quickly at the sight of him, slim and handsome in a dark blue jacket, carefully tailored pants, and an open-throated light-blue shirt that matched his eyes.

"You certainly had me fooled," he said. "Let's have a closer look." He shut the door behind him, then grasped her shoulders and turned her around as he studied her figure. "An excellent forgery. Can you do other things as well?"

"Sometimes I pass myself off as a grocery shopper," Jill responded. "I rent curlers for the occasion. And you should see my rendition of a motorist hitting the panic button when my car overheats."

Kent laughed warmly. "So you really are human after all, Jill Brandon. I sort of suspected that, but you can't be too sure. After all, I've been wrong about quite a few things these past weeks it seems."

Jill hesitated, wanting to ask him if he was certain now that he'd been wrong to suspect her of leaking the news, but she didn't want to spoil the pleasant mood. "Where are we going? Chez McDonald's?" she asked.

"Oh, a little place I happen to know," he replied, offering her his arm.

It seemed like a long drive, Jill noted as they changed from one freeway to another, but she didn't feel like questioning him further. This restaurant must be something special if he was willing to drive so far for it.

"You know, it's kind of a relief to find out I agree with a lot of your conclusions," Kent commented after a long companionable silence. "I suppose I felt threatened—don't know what I expected would happen if you were right, but feelings like that don't usually make much sense, do they?"

"I'm not sure I understand what you mean," Jill said as the freeway ended, turning into a divided road that led past the county fairgrounds.

"It was as if I had to be right, or else I was incompetent," Kent said. "What a lot of nonsense. Nobody's perfect, not even me."

"You can say that again."

"Okay. Nobody's perfect, not even me."

"What's your greatest weakness?" she probed, delighted at the chance to get to know him better when his defenses were down.

"Greatest weakness, greatest weakness," he muttered, tapping on the steering wheel. "Beautiful women in sexy dresses who let me take them out to my favorite restaurant."

"Even lady executives posing as beautiful women?" Jill prodded.

"Oh, especially them," Kent said. "I love women who pose. Even if it isn't for *Playboy*."

He swung through an interchange onto Coast

Highway and headed south. Between the low buildings on her right, Jill caught glimpses of the harbor and the last streaks of a pink and purple sunset still glimmering on the water and silhouetting the sails of hundreds of little boats.

"Peaceful, isn't it?" Kent said quietly. "I'm not much of a sailor, but somehow just looking at a sailboat helps calm me down."

"I've always wondered what it would be like to sail around the world," Jill said. "I guess I'm like you, in that if it actually came down to it I couldn't tell the aft deck from the mizzenmast, and I'd probably get seasick before we were out of the harbor. But it seems so romantic."

"That's an odd word for you to use," Kent said. "Romantic. I would think you of all people would scoff at the idea of romance."

"Oh, really?" How little he knew her! Jill thought sadly. "For your information, when I'm not stuffing my noggin full of useful information, I can sometimes actually be caught reading a romance novel . . . and enjoying it."

"That does surprise me," said Kent. "I'd like to hear more about this. Do you dream of being carried off into the sunset by a knight on a white horse?"

"That always did sound uncomfortable," she laughed. "I mean, what do they do about rest stops? I think a motor home would be a lot more practical."

Kent sighed mockingly. "Here I thought I'd discovered a whole new side of you, and what do I find? Practicality."

They turned into a parking lot, and Jill realized a small ship was docked to one side.

"The *Reuben E. Lee,*" said Kent. "Dine on deck, so to speak."

Jill was enchanted as he led her up the ramp onto the ship and discovered that the interior actually contained several different eating areas, ranging from a casual bar to a semi-formal dining room.

"You know the most wonderful places!" she said as a headwaiter led them to a table in the corner, where they could look out over the water.

"You see, it's like this." Kent held a chair for her, then seated himself. "Once in a while I disguise myself as a handsome man-about-town. Several times it has taken an entire evening for others to discover that I am in fact not human at all, but a newspaper editor."

"What sorts of things do you do to keep people from guessing?" Jill asked as she studied the menu.

"Oh, I try to order wine as if I know what I'm talking about," he said, turning to a waiter and requesting wine in perfectly accented French. "Then," he continued, "I make recommendations as if I'd tasted everything on the menu, which I have."

"What do you recommend?"

After she'd happily agreed to try a seafood dish, Kent leaned back in his seat, studying her across the table. "I'm glad things have been calming down between us. I would hate for this week to end as badly as it began."

"I seem to recall you were rather eager to get rid of me," she said.

He had the grace to look embarrassed. "As I've said before, you manage to bring out the worst in me. I've been under a lot of strain lately, and sometimes, even though I knew better, I felt as though you were the cause."

"This paper really means a lot to you, doesn't it?" she said, and he nodded. "But would it really be so terrible if you had to go to work somewhere else?"

"I've gotten used to being my own man," Kent said. "I won't pretend I've got everything I want out of life. I haven't." She remembered his adoring look when he'd played with his nephew and thought with a twinge of longing that she could guess what was missing. "But I'm past the point where I could settle for doing things someone else's way, unless I happened to agree."

"So if the worst came to pass and Arnold managed to fire you, or you felt you had to quit, what would you do?" she asked.

"I think at that point I'd be ready to try some other field," Kent admitted.

"Leave the newspaper business?" She wondered if she looked as shocked as she felt. "I can't imagine your doing anything else."

"As I say, I manage to pass for human with those who don't know me very well," he said, but despite the lightness of the words she detected a bitter undertone.

"I don't think you really want to do anything else," she said. "I hope you don't have to."

"So do I." His stern expression softened, and he reached across the table, closing his hand over hers. "What a fool I am, to sit here talking business when the moon is rising, the water is lovely, dark, and deep, and across from me sits a gorgeous woman in an almost scandalously seductive dress."

"My clothes aren't scandalous," she said with an embarrassed laugh.

"You're right," he said. "It's what they hint at underneath that's scandalous."

Her breasts tightened beneath his gaze, and she felt her nipples grow erect and warmth stir within her. Even a look and a few words from him acted on her more strongly than a whole evening of attempted seduction by other men she'd dated.

It was a relief when salads were placed before them, and Jill was able to concentrate on eating. "Is there any other line of work you've ever wanted to do?" she asked him.

"Lion taming, perhaps," he said. "Championship ice skating. Other than that, no. How about you?"

"When I was a little girl, I wanted to be a ballerina," she admitted. "Then I found out there was a lot of hard work involved, so I gave that up. At another point, I thought I'd like to be an actress, until I was in a school play and got so scared at being in front of an audience that I forgot all my lines."

"How did you get into the newspaper business?" he asked. "I don't seem to remember your ever telling me."

"It was sort of by default," Jill said, finishing up her salad. "That was before Watergate, and newspapering didn't have the glamorous reputation it's acquired since then. I kept wanting to do one thing or another in the limelight and finding out I couldn't hack it. The one thing I was good at was writing for the school paper, so I figured, why not?"

"I never wanted to be anything but an editor," Kent said, having polished off his salad while she was talking. "I identified with Clark Kent's editor rather than with Superman. It was probably my fascination with power."

"Power?"

"Yes. I love bossing people around. Hadn't you noticed?" His grin sparkled in the light of a single candle from their table.

"Now that you mention it, I believe I was aware

of that," Jill rejoined, and the two shared a smile. Perhaps it was the wine, or sheer exhaustion, or the forced intimacy of working together all day. Whatever it was, Jill decided to flow along and enjoy the evening, no matter what tomorrow might bring.

They both passed up dessert but savored their coffee while gazing out at the harbor. A yacht, lights streaming from the cabin windows, eased its way past them, headed toward its moorings.

Jill indulged in a brief fantasy of being alone with Kent on a boat, somewhere in a vast, sun-streaked ocean. They basked on deck in their bathing suits, lying side by side, surrounded by a haze of warmth and the sweet smell of sunshine on skin. He turned and ran his hand over her bare stomach...

"Daydreaming?" said Kent. "It looks like it must be pleasant."

Jill hoped the darkness covered her flush. "The harbor does make me feel romantic."

"Memories?" he asked. "Not some old boyfriend, I hope."

"Yes, in a way." She grinned up at him daringly. "Someone we both know and love."

"I'm flattered." He laid a credit card in the tray with the check and then turned to her thoughtfully. "In fact I'm so flattered I think I'll show you something few mortal eyes have seen."

"I'm afraid to ask."

He chuckled. "Nothing risqué, I'm afraid. Shall we go?"

Jill kept her curiosity in check, guessing that surprise was half the fun for him. She let him take her arm and guide her back to the car, luxuriating in his touch. The wine had gone to her head a little, and she felt marvelously free and unrestrained, delighting in the starry sky overhead and the crisp autumn air.

"I haven't felt this lighthearted since I was in college," she confessed as he held the car door for her. "I wish I could hold on to the feeling."

He swung around the car and slid in beside her. "So do I."

They headed silently back up the freeway, and then Kent began humming "Greensleeves." The poignant, ancient melody quivered through Jill's heart, and she moved closer to him.

"Now that's the effect I like a song to have," he said, encircling her with one arm.

Jill nestled against him, scarcely aware of how much time was passing, until finally she realized that they were no longer on the freeway. After a short distance the car turned into a driveway and came to a halt.

"Oh, please don't let it end," she whispered. "Why don't we go back again?"

"You can never go back, they say," Kent responded cheerfully. "But maybe what's ahead is even better."

Once outside the car, Jill was struck by the beauty of the setting. A stand of pines cut off all but the barest glimpse of other houses on the street behind them, while before her stretched one of the most striking houses she had ever seen.

It was a modern structure of natural wood with amber and ruby light shining toward her through a stunning abstract stained-glass window. The house itself seemed quite large, but because of the artful way it had been set amid the trees, it retained a feeling of intimacy.

"It's gorgeous," she said. "Absolutely beautiful, Kent."

"I wish I could say I designed it myself, but actually I just made a few suggestions to the architect," Kent said. "Of course, the best part is inside. Come on and I'll show you."

With his arm still around her, Kent led Jill into the house, and they strolled through a sleek, sunken living room and airy dining room that opened onto a central courtyard. Here an irregular-shaped pool, resembling a natural pond, meandered among bird-of-paradise bushes and camellia trees heavy with buds.

"I'm overwhelmed," Jill admitted. "This is like something out of a movie. Do you live here alone?"

Kent nodded. "I have a cleaning lady and a gardener once a week. Other than that, I can run around here any way I want without fear of giving offense."

She chuckled. "I can imagine. But when you designed it, surely you didn't intend..." She stopped as she realized what she was saying.

"Didn't intend to be the only one living here?" he finished for her. "No, I suppose not. I guess I was planning for the future."

Again Jill felt the longing she'd experienced watching Kent with his nephew. How she wished she could be the one he wanted to share his life with! But only, she corrected herself, if she could continue to be her own person.

"If you come this way, I'll show you my master-piece," Kent was saying as they walked to the other side of the courtyard and entered another wing of the house through sliding glass doors.

They were in the bedroom, Jill saw, but it was more of a suite than a single room. A giant round bed dominated the chamber, which was glowingly lit by indirect lighting. To one side a large ante-chamber opened up, and she spotted a comfort-able love seat, a small parquet table, and an arching fireplace.

"A fireplace in the bedroom!" she gasped. "Kent, I can't believe it. You really went crazy in here, didn't you?"

"There's more," he said, obviously pleased by her admiration. "Mademoiselle, *voilà.*"

She let herself be guided into the bathroom and had to admit it was the crowning glory. An oval sunken tub, lined with peacock tile, was set like a jewel into the floor.

"Here's something you don't see in your everyday run-of-the-mill tract home," observed Kent, leading her to a towel rack and running her hand over the bar.

To her amazement it was heated from within, and the towels were warm, too.

"There are solar panels on the roof," Kent explained. "It was a bit tricky with the trees, but we worked it out. It provides most of my hot water and heat and a few little luxuries like this. There's hot water running through that bar."

"I don't believe it." Jill shook her head. "How can you bear to leave all this every morning?"

"It can get rather lonely," Kent admitted. "Besides, it gives me something to look forward to when things aren't going well at the office."

"Well, I'm very impressed," she said. "I've never even dreamed of a place like this."

"Care for something to drink?" he asked. "I have a complete wet bar right here."

They adjourned to the sitting room, where Kent built a fire in the fireplace and then poured them each a shot of amaretto in hand-blown amber glasses. They rested on the love seat, bathed by the crackling heat of the fire.

"Please don't tell me you show this to all the girls," Jill said softly, rubbing her cheek against his shoulder. "You'd break my heart."

"As a matter of fact, very few are privileged enough to enter into the inner circle," Kent said. "Michael—my old boss—is one of the few, and I have some friends from my youth. Mostly I keep my private life separate from work."

"I'm glad to hear it," said Jill, thinking of Anita.

He finished his drink and set it on the table beside him. She handed him her empty glass to place beside it.

They really ought to go, Jill thought, but she couldn't bring herself to break the spell. This was a rare evening, something precious to be treasured forever, and she didn't want it to end any sooner than necessary.

Kent leaned toward her, placing a finger under her chin and tipping her face up toward him. "Your eyes are shining," he said. "Do you think that's passion, amaretto, or just reflected firelight?"

"Probably insanity," she returned.

"Mmm." He observed her with amusement. "And just how insane are you, my dear?" Before she could respond, his lips brushed against her cheek, then slid quickly and firmly to her mouth.

As she slipped her arms around him and returned his kiss with growing desire, it occurred to

Jill momentarily that she ought to draw away. It was dangerous being here alone late at night—but it was a moment that might never come again, and whatever it cost her, she couldn't bear to lose it.

Kent tasted her thoroughly, then drew slowly away, and she felt a brief pang of loss that vanished when she saw the passionate intensity in his eyes.

As the fire snapped hungrily, Kent traced the curve of her hair around her face, kissing her on the temple and then touching her ear gently with the tip of his tongue. She caressed his broad back, her hand on his shirt beneath the jacket, feeling the rippling muscles beneath.

He sat back and pulled off the jacket, draping it casually over one arm of the love seat. He sat back for a minute, studying her, and Jill's eyes half closed of their own accord. His gaze on her was like a prolonged caress, and she sensed that he could read the response in her erect nipples and the weakness that loosened her muscles, ready to receive him.

Kent was in no hurry tonight. With his forefinger he traced the pulsing curve of her throat, then slowly unbuttoned the top of her dress. Jill moaned, reaching out and touching his firm thigh as he sat beside her.

"Kent..." she whispered.

"Shhh. Don't talk." Her dress was open, revealing the creamy swell of breasts above her bra. He slid one hand behind her, and she felt the strip of cloth fall open.

Then his mouth was mastering the delicate mounds, licking, teasing, sucking. She cried out softly, leaning against him as he roused her to ecstasy.

Kent lowered her beneath him, replacing his lips with a thumb that pressed tantalizingly against the brown peaks. His mouth closed over hers again, and she responded eagerly, her tongue probing the insides of his teeth and cheeks, yearning to become part of him.

He drew away, and she lay dazed for a moment until she felt his strong arms lifting her and carrying her to the bedroom to the round bed. She was scarcely aware of what he was doing as he lowered her and removed his own clothing, so eager was she to feel him close to her again.

He sat beside her, taking in the naked swell of her breasts, the passionately parted lips, the tangle of chestnut hair. Then, with a groan, he finished opening her dress and pulled it away from her, so that she lay before him clad only in her delicate lacy underpants.

She felt the smoothness of his skin along her body as he lay beside her, flinging one leg over her so that she lay half beneath him, arching to catch his mouth with hers.

"Oh, Jill," he whispered. "You are the most beautiful woman I've ever dreamed of."

"Kent, I want you so badly," she breathed. She ran her hand down his side, feeling the sharp out-pointing hip and pulling him toward her.

"Slowly," was his response. His hands cupped her breasts, squeezing them gently together so that he could explore both at once with his mouth, his tongue licking from one taut nipple to the other.

One hand reached over and drew her panties down around her ankles, and she kicked them off. He drew her onto her side against him, their bodies pressing against each other from toe to shoulder.

Again he claimed her mouth, his hands all the while exploring the secret places of her body until she quivered against him, clutching, demanding.

He rose over her, powerful but gentle, tenderly introducing himself into her as incredible sensations shot through her body.

Jill reached down and caught his hips as if to anchor him inside her, then threw back her head and gasped as he moved back and forth.

"My love," he whispered, bending down to kiss her again. Still he prolonged the experience, proceeding with infinite patience despite the eagerness with which she pressed him to her.

Then, like a ship that yields at last to a pounding

sea, he bucked and plunged until both shuddered in uncontrollable ecstasy, crying out as sensation overwhelmed all thought.

At last the hurricane subsided, leaving him still inside her as they lay together.

"You are the most incredible woman I've ever known," Kent said. "Incredible." He ran one hand lightly over her breasts, and she trembled deliciously at the renewed stirring of desire. He laughed softly. "If only we didn't have to get up so early in the morning."

"Oh, don't remind me," Jill said. "I'll have to go home and change before work, too."

"Why don't you go just like this?" His hand pressed along her to the warmth between her legs. "You'd create quite a sensation."

"I'm sure Arnold would be impressed," she said. "Isn't this how women are traditionally supposed to get promotions?"

"Unfortunately, I've never come up against that kind of woman," Kent joked. "How come life never turns out the way it is in the movies?"

"You should complain!" She gazed over at the fire, melting down to a few iridescent embers. "This place is something out of a fairy tale."

"Not a fairy tale, please," he said. "You'll ruin my image."

Jill chuckled. "Don't worry. I'll vouch for you."

"Oh? And how will you describe this?" His kiss was lingering and thorough.

"I'd have to use a lot of purple adjectives," she murmured when he was finished. "I'm not sure I quite got the idea. Why don't you run that by me one more time?"

Laughing, Kent complied, until the two of them fell back onto the pillows, breathless.

He pulled her against him and spread the covers over them both as they cuddled together contentedly, sleep gradually quieting their breathing.

Chapter Nine

The clanging of the alarm clock drove Jill up through layers of mist into a warm cocoon where she lay in pleasant oblivion for a few minutes until something prickly rubbed along her cheek.

"Hey," she murmured, trying to brush it away and coming awake as her hand encountered Kent's shoulder.

"Like my morning stubble?" he queried. "Try this." He leaned over and kissed her. At first she felt only a tender warmth, not unpleasantly accented by the roughness of his cheeks.

Then, as their bodies moved instinctively together and he grasped her shoulders, something stirred within her. She reached up to ruffle her fingers through his hair, then pulled his head down against her breasts.

"Mmm, yes," she whispered, caressing his back.

"Whoa." Kent sat up abruptly. "Do you

know it's seven o'clock, my wonderfully lascivious friend?"

"Sev...oh, good grief!" She bolted up beside him, then sighed. "What a disappointment. I was still operating on ship's time, with no harbor in sight."

"I'm afraid the only voyage we're going to be able to make today is to the *Journal-Review*." Kent padded across the room to fetch his robe from the closet. Jill admired the broad shoulders and tapered waist and the self-possessed movements.

Reluctantly she gave up the sheltering warmth of the bed to hurry into the bathroom. Cleaning up quickly, she found her slightly rumpled dress on the bedroom carpet and slipped it on.

Kent shaved and dressed rapidly, and she marveled at the transformation from lover to editor as he stood before her in a tailored suit, his hair combed neatly into place.

"Breakfast?" he asked. "It'll have to be something quick, but I think I've got some bread somewhere."

"Do you eat breakfast normally?" she asked. When he shook his head, saying he usually just took a cup of coffee at the office, she declined the offer. "I'll have something at home. I'm not on as tight a schedule as you are."

A short time later, alone in her apartment, Jill undressed and slipped on her own robe, then fixed herself some scrambled eggs and coffee.

Gradually the contentment of the previous night ebbed away, leaving her beset by doubts.

She would certainly pay the price for one night's pleasure, she told herself as she stared glumly into her mug. Kent's thoughts had already been a million miles away on their silent drive this morning, and she had no doubt that it would be business as usual at the office.

True, she didn't live so far away as to make seeing each other impossible even after her job here was finished, but was that what he would want? In fact it might not be what she wanted, knowing that their relationship could only lead to pain and eventual separation.

A tiny seed of hope had sprouted again last night, she had to admit to herself. Perhaps there was a chance for them; they seemed so right together when they played, talked, made love.

Yet only a few days before, Kent had stood here in this very apartment, accusing her of the most outrageous behavior. It was true that he apparently had reconsidered since then, but underneath she suspected he still didn't really trust her.

Why not? Jill reviewed in her mind their experiences in Nashville, Kent's growing anger when she'd gone over his head and his refusal to concede that she'd proved her point. Try as she might to find some other explanation, she kept coming back to one point: He cared for her only when she didn't stand up for herself, only when she remained a sweet, unchallenging bit of femininity.

But femininity had another side to it: strength. A woman who had no faith in her own abilities did a disservice to her husband and children, Jill was convinced. In any sort of crisis, what kind of support could she offer them?

Most of all, she couldn't live a lie. She couldn't give all her love, all her encouragement to Kent and know that his feelings for her were conditional, that he might desert her when she needed him most.

Sadly she cleaned up the breakfast things and donned a suitably businesslike dress, then set out for the office.

Kent was already in the midst of the copy editors when she arrived, so Jill spent the morning cleaning up odds and ends. She watched a couple of reporters as they worked on their stories, then drew up her recommendations for the sports department and discussed them with Frank Rickles, who made a few suggestions but basically agreed with her proposals.

"To tell you the truth, I was kinda worried when I heard they were bringing a consultant in here," the sports editor told her. "I figured you'd change things around just for the sake of change—kinda to show who was boss."

"I certainly hope you don't think I've done that," Jill said.

Frank shook his head. "Not at all. I've been pleasantly surprised. Everything you've come up with has been a good idea. Can't understand why some people around here seem to give you such a hard time—but enough said about that."

Anita was away from her department that morning, and Jill didn't want to consult with Mary Jane yet. She suspected the Sunday editor would quickly observe how deflated she was feeling and would arrive at the truth all too quickly.

So it was a relief when Cindy popped into the conference room and asked if Jill could go to lunch.

"I'd love to," Jill said, and then realized the younger woman wore an uncharacteristically strained expression. "Still having problems with Tim?" she asked, slipping on her suit jacket and picking up her purse.

"Worse than that," Cindy said tightly. "I... Arnold gave me a couple of hours off this morning to go try to make it up with him."

"That was nice of him," Jill said as they walked out to the parking lot. "I never knew Arnold was so sympathetic to other people's feelings."

"I wish he hadn't been," Cindy answered. "I'm afraid... well, let's wait until we get where we're going. Someplace where we can have some privacy, okay?"

Jill considered where as they climbed into her Dart. "Why don't we pick up some takeout chicken and sit outside near the Independence Hall at Knott's Berry Farm?''

Cindy nodded, then fell silent as Jill drove. They stopped at the amusement park and walked through the row of shops that stood outside the main entrance. There was a tempting array of berry preserves and other delicacies offered in the glass windows, but neither woman paid them much attention.

After purchasing their chicken, they walked across the street and found a bench. Jill hoped that, whatever had happened to Cindy, she could help her friend overcome her gloom. From what she'd heard so far, this Tim wasn't worth so much anguish—but Jill knew from her own experience that all the logic in the world wasn't much use where emotions were concerned.

"I gather things didn't go too well with your boyfriend," she ventured at last as Cindy poked disconsolately at her chicken.

"Worse than that," the younger woman said.

"Broke up entirely?" Jill said. The pause that followed was so long she wondered if she should say something else, but Cindy spoke at last.

"It's even worse than that."

Jill found she didn't have much appetite for her chicken. Cindy had always seemed down to earth, so it was unlikely she was blowing things out of proportion, but what could be worse than breaking up?

"Don't tell me you're pregnant," she said.

At least that drew an amused snort from Cindy. "Oh, nothing so prosaic," she said.

"Well?"

"He told me..." Cindy stopped abruptly, then forced herself to continue. "Oh, Jill, I'm so ashamed. You'll never speak to me again when you find out what's happened."

"What have I got to do with this?" Jill asked, puzzled. "Cindy, I'm sure that whatever it is, it can't be as horrible as it seems to you."

"Did you... did you ever do anything really stupid? So stupid that afterward you couldn't believe you'd done it?" Cindy asked.

"Well..." Jill thought carefully. "Yes, one time in a story I attributed a quote to the wrong person. In fact it was the opposite of what he believed. I was in a hurry and read my notes wrong, and if I'd thought about it at all, I'd have seen the mistake, but I didn't. We had to print a retraction, and I was miserable. I didn't sleep well for weeks."

"Did you get into a lot of trouble?"

"It depends on what you mean by a lot," Jill said. "The editor was really angry and so was the man I'd misquoted, and I felt as if everyone mistrusted me for weeks. But after a while they began to remember that I'd always been accurate in the past, and when I didn't have any more foul-ups like that, they were able to accept that human errors can happen to anyone. Eventually I was even able to accept that myself, but I guess I was the hardest one of all to convince."

"I've done something even worse than that," Cindy said. "I don't even know how to tell you."

"Why don't you start at the beginning?" Jill suggested. "You and Tim got together this morning."

The other woman nodded. "I went over to his place. I was trying to work things out, but somehow we both ended up getting angry and saying things we didn't mean. Or I didn't mean, anyway."

"I know how that is," Jill said encouragingly.

"Finally I told him that he was going to have to give me more room," Cindy said. "I suppose I said it in kind of an insulting manner—that I didn't want him breathing all over me and that maybe we shouldn't see each other exclusively anymore."

"Did you mean it?"

"Yes, I did." Cindy took a sip of her soft drink. "I've changed a lot these past few weeks, for the better. I said I was growing up and becoming really professional and that he ought to do the same thing himself."

"How did he react to that?" Jill wanted to know what the terrible thing was that Cindy was supposed to have done, but the younger woman was growing tenser by the moment, and she could tell it would take some gentle sympathy to enable her to complete her tale.

"He ... he said he was a lot more professional than I was, and I had a lot of nerve telling him to grow up." Cindy's voice dropped to a whisper. "Then he said ..." She broke off.

"Have another sip of your Coke, stick your chin up in the air, and get it out of your system," Jill said. "You're making this harder on yourself than you need to."

"Okay." Cindy did as she was told and then continued in a choked voice. "He said that I wasn't professional at all, that he'd been using me for weeks, and I'd just played right into his hands."

"Oh?" Jill was beginning to get an inkling of what this might be about, but she didn't see how it could be what she suspected.

"He ... I don't know if I told you that Tim's a journalism student and he's doing an internship. You can just guess where."

Jill named the rival paper and Cindy nodded. "I think I'm beginning to get the picture," Jill said.

"He seemed so interested in everything that was going on here," Cindy said. "He would tell me about stories he was working on, and I wanted to be able to talk with him on the same level, so I would tell him about stories I'd heard about. I never guessed he was doing it on purpose."

"The leak," Jill said, wishing she could feel satisfaction in having found the evidence to clear herself, but deeply regretting that Cindy had turned out to be the innocent cause of all the trouble.

"I feel like an idiot," Cindy said. "I'd heard some talk around the office about the competition, but Arnold never said anything directly to me, so I didn't connect it with what I'd told Tim. If only I'd listened more, I'd have figured it out for myself."

"That's what they call twenty-twenty hindsight," Jill soothed. "If only I'd read my notes more carefully, I wouldn't have misquoted that man, either; but, of course, we don't realize our mistakes at the time."

"I'm going to get fired, aren't I?" Cindy said. "And the worst of it is, I deserve it. If I got fired because of something I couldn't control, or even something I could correct, like my clothes, I wouldn't feel so bad. But I've hurt everyone, the whole paper, everyone who trusted me—Kent, and Arnold, and you, Jill."

"Maybe you're making more of this than it merits," Jill said. "After all, you didn't do it on purpose."

"That's no excuse," Cindy said. "I admire you so much, Jill. I tried to be like you, to dress like you and act like you. I wanted to be so professional, and then I went and did the stupidest, most childish thing imaginable I was trying to show off for Tim, to impress him about how knowledgeable I was, and all the time he was playing me for a sucker."

"Didn't anyone warn you not to talk about stories until they were printed?" Jill said.

Cindy shook her head. "No. I guess Arnold just took that for granted. And I was so proud of the way he trusted me. He even discussed stories with me and asked my opinion. I guess he was trying to train me, to help me be more a part of the *Journal*. He's going to be so angry. Maybe I should resign and explain it to him in a letter."

"I hate to see you lose your job and that Tim get off scot-free," Jill said. "He's really the one who behaved unethically. Taking advantage of a friendship like that is not a sign of someone I would trust as a reporter."

"But he's supposed to get scoops, isn't he? His editor must have thought it was all right."

"Oh, I don't suppose there was anything so terrible about it on the surface," Jill said. "What newspaper wouldn't like to know what their opposition was planning? But the way he took advantage of his own girlfriend turns my stomach. You know, Cindy, they make a big deal on television about getting scoops, but what it boils down to is that a reporter is there to serve his community, and if he doesn't have a deep sense of fair play and responsibility, he isn't capable of doing the job properly."

"That sounds great," sighed the other woman. "But I'm afraid it doesn't excuse me."

Something in the conversation was bothering Jill, and she tried to think what it was. She went over the stories that had been leaked since her arrival—there was the case of the Siamese twins and then the Vietnamese story. It seemed to her Cindy had missed the editorial meeting where they discussed the Vietnamese story, although it might well have been mentioned to her at some other time. Still, she thought, she might as well ask.

"I seem to remember that you weren't at the meeting where we discussed the Vietnam report," Jill said. "Is that right?"

Cindy nodded. "I had a crashing headache, and Arnold let me go home early."

"How did you hear about it, then?"

Cindy looked thoughtful. "Well, I'm not sure... Oh, I guess Arnold mentioned it the next morning. He has kind of a habit of talking out loud, sort of using me as a sounding board, I guess."

"Do you remember what he said about it?"

"Um, something about wishing we weren't putting it off until Sunday, and how it was a particularly interesting story."

Jill gazed up at the replica of Independence Hall without really seeing it. A nasty suspicion was starting to form in her mind. "Arnold's been very sympathetic about your boyfriend problems, hasn't he?"

"Yes," Cindy said glumly. "That's what makes me feel even worse. I'm just dreading having to tell him what's happened."

"Maybe it won't come as such a big surprise," Jill said slowly. "Cindy, you used to talk to Tim a lot at work, didn't you?"

The other woman nodded.

"Don't you think Arnold might have overheard some of those conversations?"

"I suppose he might," Cindy said. "But surely he'd have warned me if he'd heard me discussing things I shouldn't, even though he probably didn't know where Tim was working."

"You wouldn't by chance have mentioned that fact to him at one point or another?" Jill prodded.

"I suppose it's possible," Cindy said. "Why, Jill? What are you thinking?"

"I'm not entirely sure," Jill admitted. "However I'm having a few problems with Arnold's part in all this. You could have been used by more than one person, Cindy, although I'm really reluctant to believe that. Let me give it some more thought."

"Do you think I should tell Arnold in the meantime?" the younger woman asked.

"No. I'll take care of that," said Jill. "Try not to let it get you down, Cindy. We all make mistakes, and yours was certainly innocent enough. If nothing else, Arnold should have been more cautious himself."

They returned to the paper, both lost in their own thoughts.

Jill considered discussing the matter with Kent but learned he'd gone to speak to a journalism class at a local college and wouldn't be back for several hours.

She returned to her temporary office in the conference room, working through the pages of notes she'd drawn up, but her mind was far away.

The idea that had come to her seemed incredible. She knew Arnold wanted to get rid of Kent, but would he really go so far as to arrange to have Cindy unwittingly leak the stories?

Jill searched her memory for clues. Certainly Arnold's behavior hadn't been the least suspicious when they'd discussed the Vietnamese story; in fact, he'd seemed annoyed that there was a delay in printing it. Or had that been irritation at the fact that Kent had managed to come up with an excellent report that would be difficult for the opposition to match?

She started as the telephone rang and she picked it up hesitantly. "Hello?" she said.

"Jill? Kent." It was an unexpected pleasure to hear his voice. "It occurred to me you might be expecting me to join you for dinner tonight, and I wanted to let you know I'm not going to be able to make it."

Although she hadn't given the matter much

thought, Jill experienced a sinking disappointment. "Oh, that's all right," she said.

"I'm going to be tied up with some errands, and then I've promised to have dinner with an old colleague I just ran into." He sounded impatient to be on his way.

"Kent," she said hesitantly. "I've—I may have learned some more about those leaks."

"Oh?"

"I'm not quite sure what to do about it," she said. "I have some suspicions but nothing definite. I mean ..."

He cut off her explanation abruptly. "Listen, don't worry about it. I'm sorry I accused you of being involved, and there's no need for you to try to solve the mystery."

Her own tongue seemed to be tripping her up. "I didn't mean to sound so indefinite. Do you have a minute?"

"Actually, no," he said. "I'm really in kind of a rush. Can it wait until tomorrow?"

"Sure. I guess so." Reluctantly Jill said goodbye and heard the click as he hung up the phone.

She tried to tell herself it had been considerate of him to call and let her know about dinner, but at the same time she felt hurt by his abruptness. She also wished she could have talked the matter over with him. Well, it would just have to wait.

The rest of the afternoon dragged by. Jill drew

up her recommendations for the Sunday section and went over them with Mary Jane, who suggested some refinements.

"I hope Kent and Anita go along with all these changes," Mary Jane said. "You've really come up with some winners as far as I'm concerned. I hope they can see past their own personal feelings to consider the good of the paper."

Jill considered discussing the matter of Arnold and the leaks with the Sunday editor but decided that wasn't appropriate. Although Mary Jane's advice was usually sound, this was not a matter to spread around, even to someone trustworthy. That was how Cindy had gotten into trouble in the first place, she reminded herself.

They were almost finished when Cindy came by and told Jill that Arnold wanted to see her.

"You don't suppose he's found out?" the secretary asked as they walked toward the front office.

"You're getting paranoid," Jill said. "It's probably something totally unrelated." All the same, she had to admit she felt uncomfortable herself. She didn't want to reveal her suspicions to Arnold before she'd thought them through better herself.

The silver-haired publisher greeted her with a smile so warm that she instinctively went on her guard. If there was anything she'd learned about Arnold, it was that he calculated his effects.

"I was afraid you would get everything wrapped up before I got a chance to talk to you again," he said as Cindy brought them each a cup of coffee.

Jill forced herself to relax and smile back. "Nonsense. Besides the fact that I wouldn't dream of putting together my report without running it by you, how could I resist your charming personality?"

"Now that's the kind of talk I like to hear," Arnold beamed. Cindy departed and closed the door.

"Actually I am getting pretty close to finishing the first draft," Jill chattered on, although she suspected this wasn't really what he'd called her here to talk about. "I just need to finish up the recommendations for the features section and the news department and run them by those editors, and then I'll be ready to consult with you on the overview."

"Sounds good," Arnold said. "Speaking of the news operation, there are a few things I thought we should talk about."

"Shoot."

"Well..." He hesitated briefly. "I don't want you to misunderstand this."

"Yes?"

"Yesterday, I happened to notice that you and Kent went out to lunch," he said.

"That's right, we did," Jill said, wondering where all this was leading.

"Then when I noticed how late you'd worked, I wanted to be sure you'd gotten home safely, so I called your apartment later. There was no answer."

"It sounds rather as if you'd been spying on me," she said evenly.

Arnold sighed, a bit too melodramatically. "I was afraid it would sound like that. But as I told you before, Jill, I'm concerned about you."

"That's touching, Arnold, but I don't think you asked me here to give me fatherly advice," she said.

He smiled. "You're right, as usual. Jill, I warned you once that Kent could really turn on the charm with the ladies."

"Yes, I remember that. Are you suggesting my report might be biased?"

"Oh, I'm sure your suggestions will be fine," Arnold said. "Just fine. But there are other matters that won't be in your report."

"Such as the matter of Kent's future at this newspaper?" she prodded.

"You certainly have a talent for hitting the nail on the head," he said.

Jill managed to stifle the comment that sprang to mind, about wanting to hit someone else on the head. "I'm still having a hard time figuring out exactly what you're getting at."

"Last time we discussed a certain person with Lloyd Hunter, I recall that you marshaled some strong arguments in his defense," Arnold said.

"And do you think that conversation is likely to recur?" she asked. There was no point in pushing Arnold to say whatever was on his mind. He seemed to be one of those people who prefer to manipulate others, however awkwardly, rather than level with them.

"I'm sure it will." His fingers tapped on the desk. "In discussing ways to implement your report, of course we'll be talking about personnel as well as other matters. What I'm suggesting is that perhaps your input would not be entirely objective, something I'm sure you'd agree with if you thought it over carefully."

"Wait a minute," Jill said. "I may not be a genius, but I think I'm beginning to understand all this. I'm not sure I like it."

"I hope you haven't misunderstood," Arnold said quickly.

"I hope I haven't either," she said. "I get the idea that if I speak up in Kent's behalf, you'll feel obligated to tell Lloyd exactly how nonobjective you think I am."

"I think he has a right to know all the facts," Arnold responded.

"Oh, indeed," Jill said. "Such as the facts of my personal life? That's beginning to sound suspiciously like blackmail."

"Not at all," Arnold said. "All I'm saying is that it would be better if you yourself weighed the situation and realized you might not be seeing Kent's abilities clearly. Your view might be a little, shall we say slanted, and all I'm suggesting is that if you give it some thought you'll realize that."

"And disqualify myself from defending him?" Jill asked.

"If that seems appropriate," said Arnold.

She tried to disguise her loathing as she looked at the publisher across the desk. Despite his oily assurances, it was clear to her that blackmail was exactly what he intended.

In a way, she'd certainly let herself in for it. Getting involved with Kent while she was evaluating his operation hadn't been the smartest thing she'd ever done. But no matter what her own feelings about him might be, she knew from experience and from observation that Kent was an excellent editor. And now that he'd acknowledged the need for more concentration on the paper as an integrated package, he was going to be even a better editor.

"I'll give it some thought," Jill said noncommittally, rising and leaving her half-empty coffee cup on the edge of the desk.

"Please remember that we're on the same side," Arnold said.

"I'll try to keep that in mind." She was unable to restrain a note of sarcasm as she let herself out of the office.

Cindy shot her an inquiring look, and Jill shook her head to indicate the secretary hadn't been the subject of the conversation.

It was almost five, and Jill headed out to her

car, her thoughts in turmoil. Last weekend Kent had tried to blackmail her about the leaks to force her to leave the paper, and now Arnold was threatening to tell Lloyd about her romance—however much he knew or could guess—to discredit anything she said in Kent's behalf. What a nasty underhanded business this was!

Jill drove slowly, trying to figure out what her next move should be. If she told Kent about Cindy and they went to Lloyd together, Arnold would try to make it appear that it was a scheme concocted by a lovestruck woman. Jill shivered at the thought that her feelings for Kent might become public gossip and even hurt the respect she'd worked so hard to build up in her field.

Yet what Arnold had said today intensified her doubts about him. He would go to great extremes to get rid of the managing editor. After all, it was a dangerous game he was playing with Jill; she might become so outraged by his insinuations that he antagonized her entirely, and she still had considerable clout with CCG. Surely he must have taken that into consideration and decided the risk was worth it.

You're getting nowhere fast, Jill told herself as she pulled into the parking lot at her apartment building.

Before it got any messier, she decided, it was time to get everything out in the open. Lloyd Hunter should be told what was going on—all of it—and then the decision would be on his shoulders.

Jill wished more than ever that Kent were with her now, to put his arm around her and lend moral support. Well, he'd soon be gone out of her life entirely, so she'd better get used to handling things alone, she scolded herself as she let herself into the apartment and headed for the telephone.

Chapter Ten

Lloyd didn't sound surprised to hear from her. "Got that report finished already?" he said. "I was just leaving for the day but I could drop by the *Journal* tomorrow and take a look at it."

"Actually I wasn't calling about the report," Jill said. "I found out who's been leaking the stories. The question is whether she was being used by somebody else."

"This sounds like a long one," Lloyd said. "Hold on while I get a cup of coffee."

A minute later he was settled, and she poured out the story of Cindy's breakup with Tim and Jill's own subsequent suspicions about Arnold. Then she recounted her conversation with Arnold that afternoon and admitted to having been on a date with Kent the previous night, although she saw no reason to go into details.

Lloyd remained silent for a while after she finished, and Jill ached to know what he was thinking. If he dismissed her suspicions and questioned her behavior, she could be in real trouble.

"I'll be down at the paper tomorrow morning at eight o'clock," Lloyd said finally. "I'd like to see you, Arnold, Cindy, and Kent. I'll have my secretary call Arnold's office at once and set it up."

"I'll be there," Jill said. A moment later, staring down at the phone she had just replaced on the hook, she wondered if she'd done the right thing.

That evening she felt lonelier and more desolate than she had at any time since her breakup with Kent seven years before. Her longing for his touch mingled with anxiety about the next morning's confrontation to disrupt any peace of mind she might have had. What would Arnold say? Had Lloyd already reached a decision on the matter?

Jill went to bed early and lay tossing restlessly. Kent had said that if he lost his job with the *Journal*, he might consider leaving the newspaper field altogether. What would she do if she were discredited as a consultant?

She had to concede that she didn't want to return to beat reporting with its long and frequently odd hours. Neither did she want a middle-level editing job, buried at a nondescript paper somewhere.

Yet if she lost her position now, she wouldn't have a chance of being hired as an editor at a major newspaper or as a top editor at a smaller publication.

Miserably she mulled other possibilities—law school, teaching journalism, free-lancing—none of which appealed to her. Finally, mercifully, she fell asleep.

The alarm went off at six thirty and Jill awoke already tense. She choked down her breakfast and dressed, taking more time than usual with her hair and makeup. *Might as well look my best for the execution,* she told herself with a grim attempt at humor.

She was ready early and it occurred to her that Kent might already be at the office. It might be best to alert him ahead of time, but Jill had to admit to herself that what she really wanted was to hear him reassure her that everything was going to be all right.

Driving a little faster than usual, Jill pulled into the parking lot at a quarter to eight. A handful of cars were already in the back area reserved for newsroom staff, and Kent's was among them.

Jill parked and entered through a rear door marked Staff Only. The passage led past the small lunchroom, and she glanced in idly, then froze in shock.

Standing alongside the row of coffee and soft-drink machines were Kent and Anita, their arms around each other. As she watched, Kent gave the features editor a warm hug and leaned over as if to kiss her.

Hurt and confused, Jill hurried away before they could notice her. She stopped finally to catch her breath and try to clear her thoughts.

She didn't want to believe that Arnold had been right. Surely Kent hadn't simply seduced her to win her to his side in his power struggle with the publisher. Yet hadn't he warned her in the beginning that this newspaper meant everything to him?

Resuming her walk so as not to attract attention if anyone else came by, Jill tried to make sense of what she'd seen, but the pain seared so sharply that she couldn't. It can't be what it seems; it just can't be, she kept telling herself.

A quick stop at the ladies' room gave her time to straighten her hair and get herself under control. The last thing she needed was to burst into tears in the middle of what already promised to be an extremely difficult meeting.

Cindy looked pale when Jill arrived in the outer office. "Did you know Mr. Hunter asked me to be at the meeting today?" she said.

Jill nodded. "I told him everything, Cindy. I hope you don't mind. After thinking it through, I decided it wasn't right to try to second-guess him." She kept her voice low so Arnold wouldn't overhear.

The secretary nodded. "I know. He called me at home last night and made me go through the whole thing with him. That was bad enough, but

I'm really dreading having to face Kent. I feel like I'd done something rotten to him, the way he loves this paper."

Lloyd entered and greeted both women distantly. Jill felt her stomach sink into her stockings. The fact that he wasn't acting friendly certainly didn't bode well.

They went on into Arnold's office. The publisher gave Jill a long scrutinizing look, while she tried to keep her face expressionless. Cindy, apparently eager to have something to do, prepared coffee for everybody.

Kent arrived last, and Jill tried not to think about what he and Anita had been doing in the interim. He nodded to everyone with a puzzled expression and took a seat.

"I think there are several matters here that need sorting out," Lloyd said. "I realize mornings are your busy time, Kent, but I wanted to tackle this as soon as possible."

Kent waved the objection away. "It'll be a couple of hours before things really start jumping."

If he only knew, Jill thought.

"First of all, we now know how our opposition learned what stories we were working on," Lloyd said, turning to Cindy. "Miss Selby, would you care to enlighten these two gentlemen?"

Jill stole a look at Arnold's face. He wore a quizzical expression that might have indicated he didn't know what Lloyd was talking about, or it might simply have been that he wasn't sure what this revelation was going to mean to him.

"It was my fault," Cindy said haltingly, with a pleading look at Kent. "I didn't mean to do it."

She explained about Tim and their conversations.

"I see." Kent looked thoughtful. "It never occurred to me anyone might leak the stories inadvertantly."

Arnold didn't say anything. Jill guessed that he was trying to figure out a way to turn this situation to his advantage.

"During a previous conversation that took place in this office, someone observed that the person in charge is really responsible for everything that happens under him," Lloyd said quietly.

Jill drew in her breath quickly. Arnold had said that during his attempt to place the blame on Kent for the leaks. Was Lloyd going to side with him now, or was he turning the argument against the publisher?

"I think the same point could be made here," Lloyd continued. "Cindy held long conversations with Tim from this office, and it is my understanding that she made no attempt to conceal these discussions. Is that correct?"

The secretary nodded. Jill noted that Arnold's mouth was set in a stern line.

"Furthermore, some of the information about these stories was given to her by her superior with no warning about keeping these things to herself," Lloyd said.

"If you're referring to me, I object," Arnold interrupted. "I merely talked to my secretary as any executive would and expected that anything I said to her would remain confidential, which is normal business procedure."

Lloyd nodded. "I take your meaning. But it does seem almost as though you made a point of telling her about the Vietnamese story the very day after she missed the afternoon conference."

Kent wore an expression of amazement as he stared at Arnold, but the managing editor kept silent.

"You seem to me to be implying something even worse than negligence on my part," Arnold retorted, his voice edged with anger. "Would I be wrong if I guessed that these implications were suggested to you by Miss Brandon?"

"She did acquaint me with her suspicions, yes," Lloyd said. "However, I had a long conversation with your secretary last night, and she confirmed all the key points for me."

"May I suggest that both these women have strong motivation for trying to pin the blame for this whole mess on me?" Arnold said.

"Frankly I'm not concerned with anyone's motivation in bringing this to my attention,"

Lloyd said. "I want to know if the facts as presented to me are true and if you did intentionally set Miss Selby up to leak these stories so as to embarrass Mr. Lawrence and possibly provide grounds for firing him?"

Now it was out in the open. Arnold looked pale, but he didn't give up easily.

"What you're accusing me of is a serious matter," he said. "So serious that in fact it could be considered slander."

"No one has accused you of anything, but I am questioning you, yes," Lloyd said. "It is difficult for me to know what other interpretation to put on your actions. You've made no secret of the fact that you want to get rid of Mr. Lawrence. You attempted to use the leaks as an excuse to get him fired once before. What other conclusion can I draw? But please correct me if I'm wrong."

"Of course it's wrong!" Arnold said, half rising from his seat and then apparently thinking the better of it and settling back down again. "I would never stoop to such tactics. My secretary is obviously trying to clear herself of blame for what she has done, and Miss Brandon is completely biased where Mr. Lawrence is concerned. Why, two nights ago..."

"I know all about your conversation with Miss Brandon yesterday," Lloyd said. "I am not concerned about her personal life. I'm still waiting for an explanation of how you came to discuss the

Vietnamese story with Miss Selby so fortuitously and how you managed not to overhear her frequent and lengthy conversations with her boyfriend."

"I can't believe you really set me up," Cindy put in, her voice breaking. "Maybe it is all my fault. I'm not trying to dump my guilt on you, Mr. Latimore. But it seems so . . . so coincidental, even your giving me the morning off to make up with Tim. Why should you do that?"

Arnold looked from one to the other of them, and Jill could almost hear the gears spinning in his head as he tried in vain to think of a way out. Finally he slumped back in his chair with an expression of defeat.

"What do you want, a signed confession?" he asked bitterly.

"A spoken one would be sufficient," said Lloyd. Kent still said nothing, but he was beginning to look faintly amused.

"The first leak was an accident," Arnold said. "The opposition scooped us on that Explorer Scout story, and a few days later I heard Cindy chattering away with her boyfriend. It sort of clicked. I called up the other paper and asked about him and found out he was an intern there."

"Why didn't you say something to me then?" Cindy cried.

Arnold shrugged. "I'd been looking for a way to get rid of Kent, and this fell into my lap. Don't try to put all the blame on me, Cindy; I just took advantage of what you were already doing."

"Let's leave Miss Selby out of this for the moment," said Lloyd. "Go on."

"What else is there to say? She was at the conference about the Siamese twins and passed it along. I simply failed to report her."

"But you gave her a little prod when it came to the Vietnamese report," Lloyd prompted.

Arnold nodded. "And there you have it. It wasn't as if I cold-bloodedly went about finding a way to discredit Kent, although I don't suppose that makes much difference now. It seemed like a good idea at the time."

"Is that all you have to say?"

"Only that I resign." Arnold sighed, and Jill could almost feel sorry for him. He was responsible for his own downfall, but he certainly faced a severe punishment in the marketplace, especially at his age.

"I am authorized to accept your resignation," Lloyd said. "I am also authorized to recommend a replacement as editor and publisher of the *Journal-Review,* and you might be interested to know that I intend to recommend Kent Lawrence."

"Thank you," Kent said. He was about to stand up when Cindy spoke.

"I—I resign, too," she said. "Like Arnold said, he may have helped things along, but I'm the one who's really to blame."

"That's right, you are," Kent said. "But setting up or even merely allowing such a thing knowingly and purposefully as Arnold did is one thing. Foolish, youthful errors are another. I happen to think you're turning into an excellent secretary, and I'd be happy to have you stay on, Cindy."

"Well..." the young woman hesitated.

"Don't be an idiot," Jill said. "Accept. You can give yourself twenty lashes with a wet noodle later and wear sackcloth and ashes for a week if it'll make you feel better."

Cindy managed a wan smile. "I'll stay," she said. "Thank you, Mr. Lawrence."

"If you gentlemen and ladies don't mind, I'd like to finish up a few things before I depart," Arnold said.

The others nodded and rose.

Kent and the former publisher gave each other one last, long look.

"I suppose the best man won," Arnold admitted, his mouth twisting bitterly.

"Good luck," Kent said before turning away.

Jill accompanied Kent and Lloyd back toward the newsroom. "I wish I could convince myself he's learned his lesson," said Lloyd as they walked. "I'd like to think that next time he gets a temptation like that, he'll behave more ethically."

"I'd like to think so, too, but I have a suspicion he'll merely be more careful to cover his tracks," Kent responded.

The managing editor went off to join the copy-desk, and Anita quickly engaged Lloyd in conversation, so Jill wandered into the conference room and sat down, trying to concentrate on pulling the rest of her notes together.

It was a lost cause. She couldn't seem to keep her thoughts focused on work.

Kent hadn't said anything after the meeting to apologize for his former accusations against her or the way he'd tried to drive her away from the paper. Why should he? He'd achieved his goal. The *Journal-Review* was now his to shape as he wished—as long as the results paid off in terms of subscriptions and advertisers, of course. But essentially he now had what he'd been after.

Jill still didn't want to believe that their two nights of passionate lovemaking had been nothing but a trick. Kent must have felt something for her, but whatever it was, it obviously came a weak second to what he felt for the newspaper.

Then there was the matter of Anita. What was going on between the two of them? Jill didn't think it was anything serious, but that embrace she'd witnessed certainly meant something. Perhaps the two were occasional lovers—the thought hurt so much she almost couldn't face it, but she forced herself to.

Or, more likely, now that he'd accomplished what he wanted with Jill, Kent was free to turn his attentions to a new conquest.

Oh, stop it! she chided herself. You knew there was no future together for the two of you. Why keep torturing yourself?

The most painful image of all, the one that kept repeating itself in her mind no matter how hard she tried to shut it out, was of Kent swinging his little nephew around, joy written on both their faces.

However cold-blooded he might be about the newspaper, Kent loved children dearly and must want some of his own. Surely before long he would be looking for the right woman to marry, and it wouldn't be Jill.

After more than an hour of fruitless paper-shuffling, Jill gave up. She might as well go back to Los Angeles and finish up there. She could make one more trip down to Buena Park later in the week to check her recommendations with Anita and Kent, and then it would all be done. Of course, since it would be Kent rather than Arnold who would review the whole report, she might have to face him again, but not for a few weeks at least.

Jill drove slowly home, realizing that she was going to miss the quiet community and the people she'd met there. Even Arnold. Now that it was all over, she could feel sorry for him with his mismatched marriage and his trickery. He was going to have a hard time finding another job at this stage, and his wife didn't seem like the loyal type who'd stick it out to the bitter end.

The sight of the swimming pool and whirlpool stirred painful memories, and Jill hurried up the steps into the apartment. She began to pack slowly, then paused and put in a call to her consulting firm.

She explained that she had almost completed her work and would be finishing it up at her home in West Los Angeles. Briefly she outlined the situation that had developed about the leaks and was praised for having found out the truth herself.

Jill Brandon, lady detective, she thought as she hung up the phone.

She wrote out a thank-you note to leave Lanni for lending her the apartment and asked that bills for long-distance calls be forwarded to her office.

Jill returned to her packing. Each dress seemed to carry some aching memory—the outfit she'd worn that night to the Press Club party, the bikini Kent had slipped off her in the Jacuzzi whirlpool bath, the dress she'd worn to the *Reuben E. Lee,* the ensemble she'd chosen for their outing to the amusement park.

Keep up this line of thought and you're going to have to buy a whole new wardrobe, she scolded herself as she closed the suitcase at last.

When she'd moved out to California, the idea of packing a suitcase and going on to something new had seemed refreshing and challenging. Now Jill was beginning to hate the sight of luggage.

Quit being so gloomy, she thought. One of these days you'll find the right man.

But she'd already found him. The problem was, she was the wrong woman.

The sound of the doorbell startled her. Jill walked through the apartment and opened the door.

Chapter Eleven

"You knock off work early, don't you?" said Kent with a grin, then sobered as he noticed her strained expression. "Hey, what's wrong?"

Jill couldn't think of anything to say, so surprised was she at seeing him standing here with such an easygoing attitude. "I—well, my work's nearly finished, and I—thought I might as well head on back to Los Angeles."

"What brought this on?" Kent stepped inside and closed the door behind him. "We're not in any hurry to get rid of you."

Jill made a helpless gesture with one hand. "I just—didn't want to be in the way."

"Say, what's going on with you?" Kent caught her arm and led her gently over to the couch, sitting her down beside him. His touch made Jill want to weep.

"It's only..." She looked up at him miserably.

"Oh, Kent, do we have to go through this? You got what you wanted, didn't you?"

"I think I missed out on something," Kent said. "Fill me in."

It was hard for Jill to talk through the lump in her throat. "I'm glad everything worked out so well for you. Maybe I even helped a little."

"A little, hell!" Kent said. "You helped a lot. In fact, you single-handedly discovered the leak and, furthermore, pinned it on the right culprit. Anyone else would probably have accepted that Cindy and Cindy alone was at fault."

"At least I'm glad I cleared myself," Jill managed to say.

Kent looked embarrassed. "I really owe you a big apology for that, don't I? I'm a bit slow on the uptake, but I'm beginning to see I had you figured all wrong."

"I'm glad," Jill said. "I'd hate for you to go on thinking of me that way. Who knows, we may even have a chance to work together again someday."

"You certainly are in a gloomy mood." Kent shook his head and slipped one arm around her in a gesture that intensified Jill's agony. If only the contact meant as much to him as it did to her! "You make it sound as if you were about to step on a rocket to the moon and we might see each other again through a telescope twenty or so years down the road."

Jill had to smile at that. "Not exactly," she said. "But last time we parted, you have to admit it was quite a while before our paths crossed again."

"That was different." He looked thoughtful. "You know, I'm beginning to think it's possible I misinterpreted that, too. At the time I was so hurt and angry I couldn't see straight."

"I've never understood why," she said. "All I did was go after an investigative piece and prove I could do it."

Kent shook his head. "Were you really that naive about what goes on between a man and a woman, Jill?"

"I don't know what you mean."

"The first time I got in your way, you stomped on me like I was nothing to you." His voice was harsh with emotion. "I began to think maybe our whole relationship had been a way for you to get ahead."

"But you never gave me anything because of our friendship," Jill protested. "I had to earn everything."

"I suppose so, but you certainly were making rapid progress, and part of it was that you were getting some extra-curricular instruction," Kent said.

She had to concede that he'd helped her improve her work. "But then we reached the point where you wanted to stifle me, or that's how it seemed, Kent. You wouldn't give me the same opportunity you'd have given any other reporter, as if you didn't believe I could do it!''

"Is that what you thought?" He stared at her in amazement. "That I turned down the assignment because I didn't believe in your abilities?''

"Or maybe because you wanted to keep me dependent on you," Jill said.

Kent frowned. "But that wasn't it at all."

"You couldn't have thought the exposé was a bad idea. Anyone could see that roping young country music hopefuls into prostitution was big news."

"But it was so damn dangerous!" Kent exploded. "Do you know what nearly happened to you, you little idiot? You didn't have enough sense to set things up to protect yourself! You could have been killed if they'd found out what you were up to or ended up drugged in the hold of a ship headed for Singapore!"

"I—I wasn't really thinking about that," Jill said. "I figured I could get the story."

"And you did, but you were lucky," Kent said. "The way you went about the whole thing was foolishly risky and immature. Even a seasoned reporter can get into trouble playing with people like that, and you were anything but seasoned."

"I did get scared, but everything worked out all right." Jill's voice sounded defensive even to herself.

"Yes, because I came and pulled your tail out of a sling," Kent said. "You weren't ready to handle an assignment that dangerous because you weren't mature enough to weigh the risks. Like a lot of young reporters, you jumped in with both feet first, and if you'd gotten killed and I'd approved the assignment, it would have been my fault."

"I never thought about that." Jill was beginning to feel a little ashamed of her heedlessness.

"I don't suppose it ever occurred to you either that if something had happened to you, it might have meant a lot to me personally." She looked up, startled by the intensity in his voice.

"I guess I was a lot like Cindy," she said. "Trying to prove myself and not thinking very clearly about the consequences."

"And I suppose I was thinking too much about how much I didn't want you to get hurt and not enough about your need to prove yourself," Kent admitted. "I could have worked with you on the assignment, gone over the risks with you carefully, and insisted on being kept informed at every step, but I was so hurt and angry that I couldn't even bring myself to talk about it."

"And then you left," Jill whispered, feeling again some of the desolation she'd experienced at the time.

"Just as you're leaving now?" he chided, tipping up her chin with his forefinger.

Jill nodded ruefully. "I suppose so." She halted. "But, Kent—there's something else..." The words broke off as she debated how to continue.

"Out with it," he commanded, his blue eyes staring into hers commandingly.

"This morning...I came in the back way and I happened to glance into the lunchroom and... well, I saw you with Anita," she blurted out.

He looked puzzled, then threw back his head and laughed. "You mean you caught what you thought was a passionate embrace?"

"Something like that," she said.

"You'll be happy to know that Anita is leaving the *Journal*," Kent said. "She's been hired to work in the public relations department at CCG—and she'll be associated quite closely with our friend Lloyd Hunter, to their mutual satisfaction."

"You mean you were congratulating her?"

"In my own boyish manner, yes." His hand stroked down Jill's cheek. "Frankly I thought you'd be delighted."

"That you were hugging Anita, or that she's leaving?" she teased.

"About her departure, of course. You were right about her work, as about so many things. I went through the last week's worth of her sections very carefully, and I was a bit taken aback," Kent said.

"I hope you'll find someone good to replace her," Jill ventured.

"Oh, that won't be up to me," Kent said. "As the managing editor, you'll be doing the hiring."

"I beg your pardon?" Jill wondered if she'd heard correctly.

"That's my offhand way of offering you a job," Kent said.

"As managing editor?" Jill shook her head in amazement. "I can't believe it."

"You don't have to make a decision right away." Kent's tone was serious now. "And you don't owe me anything personally if you take it, Jill."

"But why would you want me for the job?" She couldn't believe he was serious. "There must be dozens of qualified editors you could pick from, any of whom would probably give you a lot less trouble than I would."

"But I want a managing editor who can stand up to me when I'm wrong," Kent said. "And you're every bit as qualified as any other editor I could hope to find."

Jill hesitated. In many ways the move would be perfect for her. It would be a professional advancement, and she was ready for a new stage in her life—but the problem was, how was she going to adjust to working that closely with Kent, feeling the way she did about him?

"While you're thinking it over, is it all right if I use a little unfair persuasion?" Kent said huskily, leaning down to kiss her gently.

"Mmm. You can say that again," she murmured when he drew his head away.

"If you insist." He kissed her again, this time taking time to probe the corners of her mouth. Jill felt herself yield willingly as his body slid across hers on the couch.

He pulled her down beside him, and she relished the masculine firmness of his body alongside hers and the hardness of his desire.

Kent propped himself up on one elbow as he traced the curve of her neck, then bent to kiss the pulsing hollow of her throat. His lips moved slowly down her chest as he deftly unbuttoned her blouse.

Jill reached up to slip her hand inside his shirt, stroking the hairy chest, then opening his shirt and pulling him against her.

Maddeningly, provocatively, Kent toyed with her mouth, ducking away whenever her lips sought his, instead kissing the swelling tops of her breasts. Jill felt her back arch toward him instinctively, urging him on.

In a moment her breasts were bare beneath him as his tongue probed the erect nipples. She gasped, fumbling to undo his belt, feeling hot desire surge through her.

His pants joined her skirt on the floor as he stretched up to claim her mouth with his. She felt him pull the lace panties away and poise over her, stroking, licking, arousing her until she begged for him.

He entered her with the force of his desire. She cried out with pleasure, urging him on until they were both swept up on a crest of passion, moaning and sobbing as they peaked together.

"Jill, Jill." He lay over her, supporting his weight on one arm as he looked at her. "You can't go away. I won't let you."

"I know I can't," she whispered. "Oh, Kent, why can't you love me the way I am?"

"What makes you think I can't?" He sounded puzzled.

"It seems like every time I act like a grown-up instead of a clinging vine, you get angry," she said, pausing to kiss the hollow of his cheek. "Things you've said...that you prefer women like Anita..."

"Oh, Lord, did I say that?" Kent chuckled, swinging her gently up to sit next to him. "I must have been out of my mind. Jill, I got angry because I thought that in Nashville you'd just used me for your ambition."

"But I am ambitious in a way," she said. "I want to keep growing, to test my abilities, to prove what I can do."

"I don't suppose..." He stared down at his hands. "I don't suppose there's any room in there for a husband and kids, is there?"

Her breath caught in her throat. "Oh, I think there might be."

Kent looked up, hope shining in his eyes. "Jill, I want to marry you. But having a family is very important to me. I want children and a wife who would love them as much as I would."

"I could tell that from the way you played with your nephew," she said. "When I saw that, I couldn't help wishing I was the one with a loving husband and a child and another on the way. And I wished that husband were you."

His face was glowing, the look in his blue eyes so tender it made her ache. "Jill, will you marry me?"

"You'd better believe it," she said, and they both laughed.

"The job offer still holds," Kent added. "It may be a bit difficult at times keeping our business relationship out of our personal life, but I have the feeling you'll never hesitate to tell me when you disagree about something."

"In that case, I'd be happy to be your managing editor," Jill said. "There's just one thing."

"What's that?"

"We've simply got to do something about how we're handling entertainment stories!"

They both chuckled as he drew her close and they shared a long, delicious kiss.

Epilogue

"I got him!" Sarah flung the phone at the cradle and hurled herself at her keyboard. "You were right, Jill! Thank goodness for the cross-reference directory!"

As her fingers raced over the keys, the young reporter was too preoccupied with her story to notice her editor's approving nod.

Jill finished filling in a dummy drawing of Page One and pressed a button on the squawk box that connected to the composing room. "I'm sending down Page One with a hole for the lead story," she said into the intercom, then gave the computer commands to save the page dummy and send it on its way.

The intercom burped with static and then the back shop foreman's voice came across. "Got any idea when you'll be getting us that story?"

"As soon as Sarah writes it," Jill told him. "She just managed to reach one of the neighbors by phone and lucked out. The teenager who pulled the two little girls out of the fire was over there having a snack. It's worth waiting for. Don't worry. I'll leave plenty of room for a jump on Page Two. You should have enough briefs down there to fill the hole if it runs short."

"Okeydokey," came the response, and the box clicked off.

Jill glanced up at the clock. It was 1:25 A.M., five minutes short of the deadline for the Page One dummy for Saturday morning's paper.

She glanced out the newsroom window, noting how the shrill brightness around her seemed to intensify the darkness outside. Kent had questioned it at first when she'd insisted on taking her turn in rotation with all the copy editors on Friday nights, but she liked to keep her hand in. Managing editors had to stay in intimate touch with the news operation.

A slight cramp made her arch her back, and she realized vaguely that this wasn't the first time she'd felt it. Well, some things would just have to wait.

Jill bent over the computer terminal again, rapidly filling in Page Two while consulting her list of stories to be jumped from Page One. In a way she was glad the *Journal* switched from an afternoon paper to a morning one on weekends; she liked the Friday night excitement. And unlike the Sunday crew, who had a smooth and regular operation for the Saturday night shift, she faced the challenge of working with and educating often inexperienced reporters like Sarah.

Frank Rickles paused beside her and gazed over her shoulder. "Lively one tonight, eh?" said the sports editor.

"Bad fire—smoldering cigarette, they think," Jill said, sorting through photocopies of brief news items to fill in a small gap at the bottom of the page. "I can never understand people with children who don't install smoke detectors. If it hadn't been for this teenager who saw smoke coming from the upstairs and stopped his car to help, these kids would have died. The baby-sitter was fast asleep downstairs."

She felt another cramp and shifted uncomfortably in her chair.

"You feeling okay?" Frank asked worriedly. "In your condition, I'm surprised Kent lets you work."

Jill laughed. "He ought to try and stop me."

The sports editor nodded, pulling out a pack of gum and offering her a stick—which she declined—before taking one himself. "I've got to say you've whipped us into shape, Kent included, these past two years. I liked things well enough in the old days, but it's been even better since you came. And he's sure been easier to live with."

"A lot you know!" she teased, typing out a headline.

"Well, for the rest of us, anyway," Frank said,

watching as Jill finished the page and sent it to composing with a quick backup call on the squawk box. She glanced over at Sarah, but the reporter was still pounding away.

"I'd better get home before the wife starts to worry," said the sports editor, and then paused. "Heard anything new from Anita?"

"She and Lloyd sent us a postcard from Paris. What a honeymoon! All we got was a trip to an Associated Press editors' convention in Las Vegas."

"Don't sound too bad to me." He headed for the door. "And you take care now, you hear?"

"Give me another hour, and I'll take all the care I need." Jill forced herself to refrain from rubbing her abdomen and lower back, which were hurting again.

Oddly enough, the last hour of the night was a comparatively quiet time, now that all but the final story had been sent to the back shop. Jill climbed awkwardly out of her chair, feeling like a hippopotamus walking on two legs.

She strolled slowly toward the lunchroom, chuckling to herself as she recalled Kent's description of her walk as being like that of a bowlegged duck. It was lucky for him that men didn't get pregnant; she'd sure be able to think of a few jokes at his expense if he ever did!

It wasn't hard to persuade herself to indulge in a cup of coffee. Jill had been careful to eat properly and limit her caffeine the past nine months, but she was beginning to feel sleepy.

Another mild cramp gave her pause for a few seconds before she plunked her coins into the machine and retrieved the cup of hot liquid that passed for coffee. She'd had what the doctor called practice contractions for weeks now, but these did feel different. Well, her Lamaze teacher had said with a first baby it was usually about eight hours before one had to go to the hospital, so she saw no point in interrupting her work now.

Sarah had finished writing by the time Jill waddled back to her desk. She opened the story on her screen and examined it while the young reporter hovered behind her.

"I never would have thought of looking up the neighbors in the cross-reference telephone book!" Sarah said as Jill sharpened up the lead paragraph with a zingier verb. "You know, they didn't mind my calling at all, even though it was so late. They were all wired up themselves."

"You never can tell," Jill agreed. "Some people really resent having the press call, but most of them are kind of flattered." She concentrated on her editing. "Hmm. The fact that no one was seriously injured should be mentioned very high up, Sarah..."

Patiently she went over the story with the young writer, showing her how to tighten it, how to make maximum use of good quotes, and how to reorganize the facts so that the most important struck the reader first.

When she'd finished editing, Jill pressed a button and the computer told her the story's word count. Good. It should just about fit in the space she'd left for it on the page dummy.

She closed the edited article on the computer and sent it to the back shop, calling to let them know it was coming.

"You can go home now, Sarah, or you can come with me to the composing room and watch them put the paper together, if you aren't too tired," Jill said.

"Great!" cried the younger woman and bounced alongside Jill eagerly as they walked slowly out of the newsroom.

Traversing the corridor, Jill couldn't help remembering the first time she'd visited here, with Kent as a not-altogether-friendly escort. Then she'd been an outsider; now she was the managing editor, and in many ways this was her home.

There'd been changes, of course, over the past two years, from a new features editor to a new microwave oven in the lunchroom. Individuals had changed, too; Cindy, for one, had blossomed into a capable young woman, meriting several raises and increased responsibilites. Happily, Jill's friendship with her had grown, too.

The biggest change was the *Journal*'s great increase in circulation and advertising. It still fell far short of matching its better-established competitor, but the paper had won several awards as well as widespread acceptance by the public. Within the newspaper industry Jill and Kent were regarded as a canny, talented team, but they turned down all job offers. This was where they wanted to be.

Now, turning a corner toward the composing room, Jill admitted to herself that she felt a little nervous about the coming changes in her life. She and Kent had planned for this baby, attended childbirth classes together, and prepared a nursery, but she couldn't help wondering how she'd feel leaving work for six weeks—and then returning while their son or daughter would still be so tiny.

However she'd been lucky to find a competent baby-sitter just down the block from the newspaper, so she could visit with the child at lunchtime.

As if reading her thoughts, the baby kicked inside her, a little elbow protruding momentarily as a pointy lump in her side. Jill felt tears prickle in her eyes; sometimes it almost frightened her how much she already loved this little person that she hadn't even seen yet.

The no-nonsense briskness of the back shop snapped her back to the present. Pages One and Two, full-size mock-ups on boards, were all ready except for the lead story.

"They'll pull our proofs when everything's done, but we can get some of the reading out of the way now," Jill told Sarah, who was staring in fascination at the shiny strips of white waxy paper covered with black type and laid neatly in columns beneath headlines and photographs.

Partly to distract herself from the increasing twinges in her abdomen, Jill went on, explaining to the reporter the need to study the pages in overview, double-checking such easily ignored items as the date at the top, and making sure the headlines were correct.

"You wouldn't believe how easy it is to miss the most obvious things—such as a headline on the wrong story," Jill said. "There's a tendency to look right away for little typos, but it's more important to check the general picture first."

"We'll have that fire story ready any second," the foreman advised her as he walked by with the front page of the sports section, already photographed so a printing plate could be made. He slid it into a bin with the rest of the finished Saturday pages.

Sure enough, the story was done and the first two pages corrected and shot well before the three o'clock deadline. Sarah's eyes were beginning to droop, and she finally excused herself, but Jill's sympathetic gaze didn't miss the air of excitement that still animated her. Getting one's by-line on the lead story was always exciting, and this was Sarah's first time.

She will probably buy a dozen copies of the paper tomorrow and send them to all her relatives, Jill thought in amusement as she traipsed back to the newsroom to make sure the Associated Press wire machines had enough paper to last until the Sunday crew arrived that night.

"Well. I'll bet we trounced the competition with this one." Kent was sitting at Jill's desk with his feet propped up, reading a proof copy of Page One. "Sarah's turning into quite a good reporter. And it doesn't hurt that our deadline is two hours later than theirs. This fire was just being put out when they went to bed."

Jill grinned. "And let's not forget the superior editing on this paper either, shall we?"

"Oh, that." He sat upright, an amused gleam in his blue eyes. "Now you and I know that editors don't really do anything but sit around writing editorials about school boards."

Jill's chuckle was cut short by an involuntary flinch at another contraction.

"Are you okay?" His teasing manner evaporating, Kent leaped to his feet and hurried over to her. He slid one arm around her and pressed his cheek against her hair. "Are you in labor, Jill?"

"I think I might be," she admitted, allowing him to lower her into the nearest chair. "It's not that bad yet, though."

"How long has this been going on?" he demanded.

"I'm not sure." She felt the baby stir uncomfortably as the tightened muscles pressed against it. "Maybe an hour or so."

"Jill, why didn't you call me?" He sat down beside her, concern etched across his face. "I would have come in early. I could have finished putting out the paper."

"What?" she retorted. "And make you think I'm not capable of handling this job myself?"

He shook his head in amused disbelief. "Let's start timing these suckers," he said.

To her surprise the pains were coming only eight to ten minutes apart. "Almost time to go to the hospital," she said.

"A good thing you already packed your bag and put it in the car," Kent said. "I wouldn't want to take the time to go home and round up everything from washcloths to your hairbrush."

"Oh, Kent," she grumbled, "we've got lots of time."

"Yeah, sure." He rubbed her back gently, and she relaxed against his hands, welcoming the soothing massage after a long evening's work.

With Kent here, the satisfaction of having put out a newspaper yielded to the warm comfort she always felt with him, the sense of security and belonging. How strange that once she had believed him to be threatened by her competence; now she knew that he loved her completely, just as she loved him. He took pride in her work, but he would love her no matter what she did.

Another contraction racked her, and Kent finished his massage. "I say we go to the hospital right now," he ordered. As soon as the pain had passed, Jill assented.

What have I got myself into? she wondered as he helped her out to the car. *This really hurts!*

She suffered more pains during the short drive to the hospital. Fortunately they had preregistered, and Kent only had to spend a few minutes in admitting while she was placed in a wheelchair, taken up to the maternity ward, and changed into a hospital gown.

The labor room was drearily impersonal, but the nurses spoke to Jill encouragingly, and Kent joined her within a few minutes. They'd practiced their breathing techniques, but it was different now: Instead of giggling and joking between pretend contractions, she found herself in a deadly serious mood.

Her whole body seemed to ache, and her heart went out to the little baby, so rudely shoved about. When the contractions peaked, it was a struggle to keep from feeling helpless and out-of-control. Only Kent's soothing voice, reminding her to focus on her breathing and relaxation, kept her on track.

"You're progressing rapidly for a primipara—a first-time mom," said one of the nurses after checking on them. "I'm going to call in your doctor."

"There's no need to set a speed record," Kent advised Jill. "There aren't any deadlines, you know, and I doubt if the competition will scoop us on this one."

She managed only a weak smile before the next contraction hit. From there on it seemed as if one wave of pain barely crested before the next one hit.

"Try to keep calm," murmured Kent's voice through her fog of pain. "This is what our teacher called transition, remember? It's nearly over now."

Afterward, she never could remember being wheeled to the delivery room—only the sudden sense of relief when the nurse told her to go ahead and push. Minutes later, an angry baby's cry burst through the hushed voices of the medical staff.

"It's a girl!" someone said.

"Melissa," Jill whispered, the name she and Kent had agreed upon after hours of discussion.

"Boy, is she a beauty, just like her mother!" Kent chortled. "A little messy at the moment, but wait'll you see those big eyes!"

Someone placed the baby on Jill's stomach, and Kent helped her lift her head.

Peering back at Jill was a pair of bright, curious blue eyes. The rest of the baby was covered with a mixture of blood and a white waxy substance, as they'd been told in class that it would be, but it was the intelligent expression that held her.

"A little reporter," Jill said. "Look at her, Kent. She's trying to figure out what kind of story to write about all this."

One of the nurses picked up Melissa and carried her to be bathed while Kent leaned over and hugged Jill tenderly.

"I love you," he said. "And I love our daughter."

Jill could only nod, tears in her eyes. "She's perfect, isn't she?"

He grinned. "Haven't counted all the fingers and toes yet, but if she has flaws, I'll love those, too. Just as I love yours."

"What flaws?" Jill retorted. "Besides being crazy about you?"

"Working yourself half to death," murmured Kent. "But let's not argue."

"Pooh." Weary but determined not to let him have the last word, Jill glanced at the clock. It was eight o'clock in the morning. "I can catch a few hours sleep and get back to the paper in time to make sure the Sunday operation is going smoothly."

"Oh, no, you..." He stopped as he realized he'd been had. "Okay, you win. No flaws. Except being crazy about me." He stroked her rumpled hair and gazed down at her, love glowing on his face. "And that's one flaw you'd darn well better hang on to."

"Oh, I think I might," she said, already half

asleep as she was wheeled down the corridor to the recovery room. But even as she dozed, suddenly and completely exhausted, she felt a physical awareness of Kent hovering beside her, protecting her as she slept.

HARLEQUIN *Love Affair*

Now on sale

MIX AND MATCH   *Beverly Sommers*

Scott Campbell may have looked like a surfer, Ariel thought, but he could never have been a good one. Scott seemed to be as blind as a bat. Why else would he bypass the bikinied denizens of Seal Beach, California, to make a play for a woman who was almost middle-aged? A woman whose teenage daughter cast disapproving glares at him and whose younger daughter skulked around him menacingly, distressingly attired in combat fatigues.

True, Ariel respected Scott's advice—he had improved both her painting and her business. But anything more than a friendly relationship was unseemly. Preposterous. And so appealing. . . .

THE DREAM NEVER DIES   *Jacqueline Diamond*

Consultant Jill Brandon walked into the offices of the Buena Park newspaper and received two rude shocks. One was Kent Lawrence, the paper's managing editor. As Jill tried to revamp the daily, Kent dogged her footsteps, hurling the same bitter accusations she had heard from him years before. Kent Lawrence had not forgotten her one rash act as a young reporter, an act that had launched her career and ruined their relationship. Nor had he forgiven her for it.

That was the first shock—that Kent still despised her. But the second shock was much worse. After all the years, Jill still loved him.

MISPLACED DESTINY   *Sharon McCaffree*

Carla didn't recognise him at first—after fifteen years, Brigg Carlyle had changed. But the atmosphere at the Shelbyville reunion catapulted Carla into the past, and she found herself responding to Brigg as though he were still her best friend's obnoxious older brother.

Brigg didn't like that. And after the reunion, in Chicago, Brigg made Carla realize that the fireworks that still erupted between them were now the result of adult emotions, not youthful high spirits. Brigg loved her. He had always loved her. But Brigg was no longer the familiar boy of Carla's past—he was a man, and a stranger.

HARLEQUIN *Love Affair*

Next month's titles

STARSTRUCK   *Anne McAllister*

Any man who attempted to turn an interview into a seduction, then had the nerve to invite himself to dinner, deserved exactly what he got. Liv James couldn't help feeling that actor Joe Harrington, America's heart-throb, deserved a good dose of reality—Liv's kind of reality. That included a hyperactive rabbit cavorting in the back of her van, a slightly charred casserole and, of course, the children.

Five of them. If the casserole didn't poison him, the commotion would deafen him. . . . It must have been the novelty he loved, Liv decided. But as time passed and Joe began to talk of settling in Madison, Liv prayed the novelty would wear off before she got in too deep!

SEASON OF DREAMS   *Robin Francis*

It was ironic that the Stratford, Oregon, Centennial Celebration was to be held at the Warwick Inn. The old hotel had been recently purchased by Domini Developers and was to be decorated by Sommers Nurseries. Once, Thia Sommers and Luc Domini had been outsiders in the town, and both had fled after high school. Thia's love of plants had called her home to take over her grandmother's nurseries. But Luc Domini had become the kind of successful, polished businessman who usually buried an unhappy past.

His return mystified Thia—until she learned that he had come back for her!

THE GLORY RUN   *Anne Henry*

Once Emily Williams had been a fleet-footed golden-haired girl who existed for the sheer joy of running. Despite her eight-year hiatus from competition, coach Keith Lancaster had only to see Emily on the track to know that she still possessed the heart of a runner and the grace of a gazelle. Once Emily had been the Texas state champion. With Keith's help, she could be the best in the world.

But time had changed Emily, endowing her with a woman's heart. She needed much more than determination and his help to win. She needed Keith's love.